WITHD

SAM WU
is <u>NOT</u> afraid of
SPACE

EGMONT

EGMONT

We bring stories to life

First published in Great Britain in 2020
by Egmont UK Limited
2 Minster Court, London EC3R 7BB

Text © 2020 Katie Tsang and Kevin Tsang
Cover illustration © 2020 Nathan Reed
Interior illustrations by Dynamo © 2020 Egmont
Illustrations on p59, 133 and 161 by Olivia Adams, Illustrations on
p. xii, 4, 5, 9, 10, 12,13, 22, 23, 59, 74, 80,111,114,115, 133, 135, 138,
139, 140, 142, 147, 151, 161, 184 © Nathan Reed
ISBN 978 1 4052 9761 5

www.egmont.co.uk

A CIP catalogue record for this title is available from the British Library.

Printed and bound in Great Britain by the CPI Group

70931/001

All rights reserved. No part of this publication may be reproduced,
stored in a retrieval system, or transmitted, in any form or by any means,
electronic, mechanical, photocopying, recording or otherwise,
without the prior permission of the publisher and copyright owner.

Stay safe online. Any website addresses listed in this book are correct
at the time of going to print. However, Egmont is not responsible
for content hosted by third parties. Please be aware that online content
can be subject to change and websites can contain content
that is unsuitable for children. We advise that all children are
supervised when using the internet.

MIX
Paper from
responsible sources
FSC® C020471

SAM WU

is NOT afraid of SPACE

KATIE & KEVIN TSANG

Illustrated by Nathan Reed

FOR THE CAPTAIN AND COMMANDERS
OF THE SAM WU SERIES:
OUR EDITORS LINDSEY HEAVEN
AND ALI DOUGAL
AND OUR AGENT CLAIRE WILSON
–Katie and Kevin Tsang

CONTENTS

CHAPTER 1

THE SCARIEST THING IN THE UNIVERSE

My name is **Sam Wu** and I am <u>**NOT**</u> afraid of space. And by that I mean outer space. With stars and planets and aliens and moons and spaceships.

I may not have *actually* been to space yet, but I've done the closest thing.

I've been to **SPACE CAMP**.

You might be wondering what is so scary about space.

Let me tell you. There is an **ENTIRE** universe of scary things out there in space . . .

SCARY THINGS IN SPACE:

No gravity so you might just float through space **FOREVER**.

Aliens.

Exploding meteors.

SUPER gravity so you might get smushed into the ground.

Black holes.

No oxygen.

Freezing temperatures. Like so freezing, your entire body can turn into an ice cube.

Your brain getting sucked out through your nose.[1]

[1] I'm pretty sure this is what happens if astronauts take off their helmets in space. I haven't actually seen it.

AND, ON TOP OF ALL THAT, SPACE GHOSTS.[2]

I found out about all these things at Space Camp. And it was there that I had to prove how **NOT** afraid I was. I've had to prove how not afraid I am over and over again. I've faced ghosts, sharks, the dark, spiders, even zombies. But little did I know that all that was just to prepare me for all the scary things in

SPACE! !//

[2] Space ghosts are ghosts that float around in outer space. Way scarier than normal ghosts here on Earth.

CHAPTER 2

WHO DOESN'T LOVE SPACE BLASTERS?

It all started, as so many things in my life do, with . . .

SPACE BLASTERS is not only my favourite TV show, it is the **BEST** show in the universe. I've been watching it **FOREVER**. I'm definitely its number one fan. It is about **Spaceman Jack**, **Captain Jane** and their alien friend Five-Eyed

Frank, and the adventures they have all over the universe! I would do *ANYTHING* to be a spaceman.[1]

Ask ANYONE.[2]

Sometimes, you don't even need to ask me, I'll just start telling you how great **SPACE BLASTERS** is.

I was doing just this at school one day with my

best friends, **Bernard** and **Zoe**. They are used to me talking a lot about **SPACE BLASTERS**.

But then, just as I was quoting **Spaceman Jack** (he's my favourite character on the show), **Ralph Philip Zinkerman the Third** showed up.

[1] A spaceman is kind of like an astronaut but even COOLER.
[2] By anyone, I mean you should ask me.

Ralph and I have an **interesting** history. We were former enemies (after all, he was the one who started calling me Scaredy-Cat Sam in front of the **WHOLE** class and the reason I had to start proving how brave I was in the first place)

SPACE BLASTERS

but after surviving **MULTIPLE** life-or-death situations together, we were almost friends. I guess coming face to face with zombies will do that for you.

He still wasn't a fan of **SPACE BLASTERS**.

'Are you talking about that space show **AGAIN**?' Ralph said. 'I don't get what is so great about it.'

'That's because you've never even seen a **SINGLE** episode!' I said. 'I bet if you watched one you would be a fan too.'

I was expecting Ralph to snort (this is his signature move) but instead he shrugged. 'Okay,' he said. 'I'll watch an episode.'

And that is how Ralph ended up at my house watching **SPACE BLASTERS**, which then led to us going to Space Camp, and me having to prove how brave I was. Again. But that was all to come . . .

Here is what you need to know about Ralph:

1. He can be **THE WORST**, but he's a good person to have on your side.
2. He **SNORTS** at basically everything you say to him. He is the master of snorts.

3. He loves **BOW TIES**.

4. He has a twin sister named **REGINA**.

Here is what you need to know about his twin sister Regina:

   1. She's way nicer than Ralph.

Ralph and Regina had only been to my house once before, and that was on Halloween and for a **VERY** short visit.

This was different. This was going to be a whole night at my house. Everything had to be PERFECT. What if they didn't like SPACE BLASTERS? I'd NEVER live it down!

Zoe and Bernard helped me prepare.

'You need snacks,' said Zoe. 'Lots of snacks. Lots of really good snacks.'

'Sam always has good snacks,' said Bernard. 'Like those prawn crackers. Do you have any of those by the way?'

'Of course I have prawn crackers. We always have prawn crackers! But Zoe's right. We need **LOTS** of snacks.'

'Popcorn,' said Zoe. 'You definitely need popcorn for a **SPACE BLASTERS** marathon.'

'I'll ask my mum for popcorn,' I said. But I still felt anxious. I must have looked anxious too because Bernard patted me on the back.

'Don't worry, Sam, they'll love **SPACE BLASTERS**,' he said. 'Zoe and I liked it right away, remember?'

'You're right,' I said, trying to sound more confident than I felt. 'Everyone loves SPACE BLASTERS.'

When the doorbell rang, I had all the snacks set out and my favourite episodes of SPACE BLASTERS lined up on the TV. We were ready to go!

Of course my little sister Lucy got to the front door first, wearing her cat pyjamas and clutching her cat Butterbutt in her arms.

'WELCOME! I am

QUEEN LUCY

and THIS is my castle!'

'Hello, Queen Lucy,' said Regina, curtsying. For someone who didn't have a little sister, Regina knew exactly the right way to handle them. 'May we come in?'

Lucy grinned at her. 'What's the password?' she said.

'Lucy is the queen,' Regina said quickly.

'Correct!' declared Lucy, spinning around. 'You may enter!'

'Hi, guys,' I said to Ralph and Regina. 'You ready for the **BEST** TV show ever?'

'I have very low expectations,' said Ralph, sitting down on the sofa and grabbing a handful of popcorn.

'I know it is going to be great,' said Regina, sitting next to Zoe. 'From everything you've said about **SPACE BLASTERS**, it sounds **AWESOME**.'

'I hope you like it,' I said, and pressed play.

☆ 🚀 ☆

Two episodes later, Ralph and Regina were hooked, just like I knew they would be.

'Everything looking good for take-off, **Captain Jane**?' said **Spaceman Jack**.

'All clear,' said **Captain Jane**.

'Nooo! It's not all clear!' said Zoe. 'The Ghost King is ON the spaceship!'

Suddenly, the lights flickered and went out. The TV turned off with a . . .

I wanted to yell for my mum, but I didn't want
Ralph and Regina to think I was afraid.

'Everybody, **STAY CALM!**' I said.

Ralph turned on the flashlight on his phone. 'I am
calm,' he said. 'You don't sound very calm though.'

'I think this is a **SITUATION**,' I said.

'Sometimes the lights just go out. That
happened before, remember?' said Bernard.

'Yeah – when we were watching a **SPACE
BLASTERS** episode about **THE GHOST
KING!** A coincidence? I think not!' I declared.

Ralph started to look nervous.
'What do you mean, it happened before?'

'I think the Ghost King is here on planet
Earth,' I said. I lowered my voice. 'Maybe even
IN this house. He's looking for something.
Or someone.' I looked at my friends. 'This is
SERIOUS. More serious than zombies. Or the

last time we faced the Ghost King.'

'The last time?' Ralph yelped.

'We dealt with it, don't worry,' said Zoe. 'We have the certificates to prove it and everything.'

'How do we know if the Ghost King is here?' asked Regina, looking around the room as if she might have been able to see the Ghost King.

'There will be **CLUES**.' I pointed at the TV. 'Like on the spaceship on **SPACE BLASTERS**. The power goes out, then things start to go missing – all signs of the Ghost King.'

'I don't believe the Ghost King is real,' Ralph said very loudly. In the kind of way that made me think he probably **DEFINITELY** believed the Ghost King was real . . .

PHEW! The lights came back on and the TV did too. **Spaceman Jack** was talking. 'It's important to be on high alert,' he said.

We all stared at each other. 'You hear **Spaceman Jack**,' I said. 'We all need to be on high alert!'

We finished watching the episode, and the power stayed on the whole time. At the end credits, Ralph turned to me. 'You know what, Sam,' he said slowly, ' **SPACE BLASTERS** wasn't as terrible as I was expecting it to be.'

'It was **AMAZING!**' said Regina. 'I loved it. **Captain Jane** is the best. She flew TUBS[3] through a whole moon **LABYRINTH!**'

'She's really good at flying spaceships,' I said proudly.

---

[3] TUBS stands for The Universe's Best Spacecraft and is the name of the spaceship on **SPACE BLASTERS**.

'And that alien space battle on Planet Zonkers?' said Ralph. 'That was **SO COOL!**'

'I want to be just like **Captain Jane**,' said Zoe.

'You really, **really** love space,' said Ralph, still looking at me. I thought he was making fun of me at first, but he seemed serious. I nodded.

Ralph and Regina suddenly looked at each other over my head, and appeared to be having a conversation with their eyes. It must have been a **TWIN THING**. Then they both started to grin at the exact same time.

17

'I've got the **BEST** idea,' said Regina, her grin growing even wider.

'No,' said Ralph. '*We've* got the best idea.'

'We're going to Space Camp,' said Regina. 'All of us.'

CHAPTER 3

HOW TO PACK FOR OUTER SPACE

'<u>SPACE CAMP</u>? Actual real **Space Camp**?' I spluttered. Going to **Space Camp** was my biggest dream.

'Yep,' said Regina with a huge smile. 'We're going over the Christmas holidays.'

'Didn't you already go last summer?' Bernard asked Ralph.

'The summer session was cancelled,' said Ralph. 'And **of course** you are going, Sam. I said you are going. So you are going.' He looked at Zoe and Bernard. 'You two are coming too.'

'Are you going to sneak us there in your suitcase?' said Zoe sceptically.

Ralph scoffed. 'Obviously not. We'll just ask our parents to send all of us.' He said this as if it was no big deal, even though it was a **VERY BIG DEAL**.

'Exactly!' said Regina. 'Easy-peasy.'

Zoe, Bernard and I just sat staring at them.

'Even if you convince your parents to send us to Space Camp,' Zoe said slowly, 'how are you going to convince our parents to let us go?'

'We'll take care of it. Trust us,' said Ralph.

☆ 🚀 ☆

I should have known Ralph was good at getting what he wanted. Because not only did he and Regina convince their parents to send all five of us to Space Camp, his parents convinced my parents to let me go! Even though it was for a **WHOLE WEEK**.

It was all happening. I, Sam Wu, official SPACE BLASTERS' number one fan and future spaceman, was going to Space Camp. All that was between me and what was surely going to be the **BEST WEEK OF MY LIFE** was packing my space bags[1].

---

[1] Technically just my suitcase, but from here on, it was a space bag.

On the morning we were leaving for
SPACE CAMP, I made
sure I enjoyed my breakfast
of congee[2] and the fresh
orange juice my dad had squeezed.

'I'm proud of you, Sam,' said my dad as he
poured me more orange juice. 'You've come a long
way with Ralph. I remember when he was the last
person you would want to go away with, but look
at you two now, the best of friends!'

'I wouldn't say "the best of friends",' I said,
but my dad ignored me.

'And going to Space Camp! It's very generous
of the Zinkermans to send all of you.'

'Felicity Zinkerman was telling me that her
family is one of the key donors to the camp,'

---

[2] Congee is a rice porridge and it is my FAVOURITE breakfast.
Na-Na, that's my grandma who lives with us, makes it for me almost
every morning. I didn't think they'd have congee at Space Camp.

said my mum, taking a sip of her tea. 'So the camp was more than happy to have her kids and their friends come to stay.'

I wasn't exactly sure what that all meant but I knew what the result was: I was getting to go to **SPACE CAMP** and it was paid for.

'I'm going to miss you,' Lucy announced, kicking me under the table.

'I'm going to miss you too, Luce,' I said, kicking her back. 'But you'll look after Fang and Butterbutt while I'm gone, right?'

Fang is my **VERY** fierce man-eating[3] pet snake.

---

[3] I have not yet seen Fang eat a person but one day he might.

Only the **BRAVEST** people can hold Fang. Like me. And Lucy, who is incredibly brave for a little sister.

'Of course,' said Lucy. 'We're going to have **LOTS** of adventures while you are at Space Camp.'

I grinned at her. 'Okay, I want to hear all about them when I get back.'

'You be good at Space Camp,' said Na-Na. 'I won't be there to get you out of any trouble,' she added, waggling her eyebrows at me. Sometimes, when I get into a little bit of a **SITUATION** and need a grown-up, my Na-Na will let me bargain with her for help. In return I usually have to weed her garden.

'Don't worry about me,' I said to Lucy. 'I'm going to be the **BEST** astronaut-in-training that Space Camp has ever seen!'

CHAPTER 4

READY FOR TAKE-OFF

From the outside, Space Camp did not look **anything** like how I thought it would.

Even though I knew we weren't **actually** going into space, for some reason I had imagined camp would at least be up in the air.

It was not. It was a huge square building with no windows. And it was one hundred per cent on the ground.

Zoe clearly felt the same way I did. 'Are you sure **this** is Space Camp?' she said. 'It's nowhere near space!'

'It says "Space Camp" right there,' said

Bernard, pointing to the side of the building where

was clearly written.

'I bet the **WHOLE BUILDING** takes off into space,' said Regina. 'Just wait.'

I swallowed. I wasn't totally sure *that* was what I wanted either.

We all stared up at it.

'Hurry up, children,' said Ralph and Regina's mum, bustling behind us. 'You don't want to miss take-off,' she said with a laugh.

'**SEE?**' said Regina. 'I knew we'd be taking off somewhere!'

☆ 🚀 ☆

Once we were inside, it seemed to grow a **MILLION** times bigger. I'd never been in such a humongous building! And everything inside it was **AWESOME**. I didn't know where to look first!

Even though it was daytime outside, just inside Space Camp building, it was like stepping into the starry night sky. I couldn't even tell where the walls were – when I looked for them I could only see stars on an night sky that seemed to go on forever.

No wonder it was such a big building! It wasn't going up into space – they'd brought space down to Earth!

In the centre of the room was what looked like a giant hamster enclosure made of connecting tubes and squares.

'I think that's meant to be the space station,' whispered Regina next to me, pointing at it. 'It's where we sleep!'

I gulped. I'd forgotten that I was going to be **SLEEPING** here.

'Welcome, future astronauts!' boomed a voice over the loudspeaker. *'Please immediately report to Area One to sign in and get fitted for your spacesuits.'*

'This is where I leave you,' said Mrs Zinkerman, checking her phone. 'Ralphie, Regina, come over and give me a kiss goodbye.' She leaned down and Ralph and Regina dutifully kissed her on the cheek. 'Farewell, my dear space explorers! I can't wait to hear all about your intergalactic adventures!'

And then she was gone.

'Future astronauts, please immediately report to Area One,' the voice repeated over

the loudspeaker.

'That's . . . us,' I said, not quite believing that we were the **future astronauts**. 'Let's go!'

We joined a group of kids and stood at the back.

'I think we're the youngest ones here,' said Zoe, looking around.

As if he had heard her, a tall boy with a big nose turned around and glared at us. 'Ugh. Who invited a bunch of babies?'

Ralph bristled next to me.

Zoe crossed her arms and glared back at the tall boy. 'I bet we know way more about space than you do.' Zoe has older siblings and isn't intimidated by **ANYONE**. She pointed at me. 'My friend Sam is a space expert.'

I tried to look serious, like a space expert would.

'Yeah!' said Regina. 'Nobody knows more

about space than Sam!'

I gulped.

'Oh yeah?' said the tall boy. 'This is my third year at Space Camp. I'm pretty sure I know more than you do.' He looked at me a little closer and then started laughing. 'Where did you get that shirt? Looks stupid.'

I was wearing my special **SPACE BLASTERS** shirt that I'd made myself.

'You clearly know nothing,' said Ralph, pushing forwards and glaring up at the boy. 'That is a one-of-a-kind **SPACE BLASTERS** shirt.'

'What the heck is **SPACE BLASTERS**?' said the boy.

'The **BEST** TV show in the universe!' I burst out.

'Yeah!' added Bernard. 'Everyone knows about **SPACE BLASTERS**.'

'You kids are weird,' said the boy, turning back around. 'Just stay out of my way.'

'You stay out of **OUR** way,' said Zoe.

'Zoe,' I whispered, 'maybe we should just stay out of his way.'

'Attention, space cadets!' said a woman at the front with black hair that sat on her head like a helmet. 'Attention and welcome to the winter session of Space Camp. We're so glad everyone was able to join us. I'm Commander Margaret Liu, and these are my colleagues, Commander Wes Herman –' she pointed at a short man next to her with curly hair like Bernard – 'and Commander Sharon Hopper.' A tall woman with lots of small braids smiled and waved at us. 'We'll be leading you on your missions this week here at Space Camp.'

'And yes,' said Commander Sharon, 'we've all really been to space.'

We all applauded.

I couldn't believe that I was meeting **real life astronauts!** Going to Space Camp was by far the coolest thing I'd **EVER** done!

'You'll be split up into teams of six,' said Commander Margaret. 'Throughout the week you'll compete against other teams in four challenges as well as learn what it takes to be a real astronaut.'

'Sam,' said Bernard in a low, urgent voice. 'There are only five of us! Who is going to be our sixth person?'

'As long as it isn't that guy,' said Zoe, looking at the tall boy in front of us, 'I don't care who it is.'

'First up, we have Team Red. Please listen out for your names,' said Commander Margaret. She started reading out names. When she said,

'Felix Stevenson,' the boy in front of us stepped forwards.

'I hope we aren't on different teams,' I said, starting to get an anxious feeling in the pit of my tummy. That thought hadn't even occurred to me!

Commander Sharon read out Team Yellow.

None of our names were listed.

Then Commander Wes read out Team Green.

I held my breath the whole time. Not a single one of our names were called.

'We are at the right camp, aren't we?' said Bernard.

I nodded. At least I hoped we were.

'This is good,' I said. 'It means we're all on the **SAME TEAM!**'

'And last but not least, we have Team Blue,' said Commander Margaret. 'First is Sally Doyle . . .'

'She'd better say one of our names next!' said Zoe.

'She'd better say *all* of our names,' I said.

'Shh!' said Ralph. 'Listen!'

'Zoe Turner . . . Bernard Wilson . . . Sam Wu . . .'

When she said my name after Zoe's and Bernard's, I smiled so wide it made my cheeks hurt.

'And Ralph and Regina Zinkerman,' finished Commander Margaret.

The five of us cheered, and Commander Margaret laughed.

'I like your enthusiasm,' she said.

I looked around. Who and where was Sally Doyle?

'Do I have to be on a team?' said a girl with two long red braids and about a million freckles who was smacking on pink bubblegum. She blew a giant bubble, almost as big as her face, and popped it with her finger. 'I'm not really a team player.'

'That must be Sally Doyle,' Bernard said.

'Yes, Sally, you have to be on a **TEAM**,' said Commander Wes with a smile. 'Just like we all have to be on a team when we go up to the International Space Station. No single person can run an entire spaceship by themselves!'

'Bet I could,' Sally said, with another smack of her gum.

'I'm Sam,' I said. I tried to think of what **Captain Jane** would say in this situation. 'It's, erm, an honour to have you on our team, helping us with the challenges.'

'I don't care about silly fake space challenges,' said Sally. 'I don't even want to be here. My parents made me come.' She rolled her eyes.

'Can we swap her out for a different teammate?' whispered Bernard.

I took a deep breath and tried not to think

CHAPTER 5

EVERYTHING IS A MISSION AT SPACE CAMP

After we had been divided into teams and given our uniforms for the week (I couldn't believe we actually got to wear **OFFICIAL SPACE CAMP UNIFORMS!**) we went to find our sleep pods. We went inside one of the huge tubes that snaked around the building. It was modelled on the real International Space Station!

'It's just like being on an actual spaceship!' I said, practically skipping through the halls. It was just me, Ralph and Bernard. Zoe and Regina

had gone to find the corridor where the girl
astronauts slept.

'Except we're still on Earth,' said Ralph.
I ignored him. I knew he thought it was cool.

How could he not? It was hands down the coolest place I had **EVER** been.

Bernard was staring at the map and guiding us. 'Okay! Turn left up here . . . oh wait, I think

I mean turn right.' He frowned and held the map upside down. 'It is impossible to tell where we are on this map!'

'Give me that,' said Ralph, snatching the map out of Bernard's hands. 'It's **THIS** way,' he said, pointing down a dark corridor up ahead of us.

'Are you sure?' asked Bernard.

'I'm always sure,' said Ralph. 'Now come on, I want to see these bunk beds. I can't believe I have to share a room with you two.'

As we went down the dark corridor, lights flickered on above us.

'Motion sensor lights,' said Bernard, sounding impressed.

'This **IS** Space Camp,' I said. 'I'd expect nothing less!'

'You two get excited about the weirdest things,' grumbled Ralph. Then he pointed. 'Look,' he said. 'Room 405B. That's us.'

We pushed the door open and froze.

It was Felix. 'What are you babies doing in here?'

'This is our room,' I said, trying to sound brave.

'It is not,' said Felix. 'The pipsqueaks get the smallest rooms. These rooms –' he threw his arms out wide – 'are for the older, more experienced space cadets. Now get out of here.'

Ralph somehow managed to sneer up at Felix, an impressive feat. He thrust out our yellow folder. 'We're in room 405B,' he said. '*See?*'

'Go and look outside at the number on the door,' said Felix smugly. 'You'll find this is 504B.'

'Oh,' said Ralph, turning brighter red than I'd ever seen him. He looked at me and Bernard. 'Why didn't you guys say something?' he said.

'We were following you!' said Bernard. 'You took the map!'

'Can you three miniature musketeers go argue about this somewhere else?' said Felix. 'Some of us have important space work to do.'

Bernard, Ralph and I shuffled out of the small room. Felix slammed the door behind us, leaving us in the corridor.

I took a deep breath and looked between my best friend and my former nemesis, now friend. Someone clearly needed to take charge.

'That was just a slight hiccup,' I began.

'Nobody hiccupped,' said Ralph with a scowl. 'We got lost.'

'It's an expression,' I explained.

'It means a small thing went wrong,' added Bernard.

'I **KNOW** what it means,' huffed Ralph.

'Anyway, as I was saying,' I said, raising my voice a little, 'that was a slight hiccup, but don't worry! We won't be deterred from our mission!'

Both Ralph and Bernard stared at me, confused expressions on their faces.

'What mission?' asked Bernard.

'The mission to find our sleep pods!' I said.

Ralph groaned. 'I forgot that you treat **everything** as a mission,' he said.

'Well, we are at Space Camp! Everything **is** a mission. Let me look at that map.'

Eventually, we found our way to room 405B.

It was very, very, very small.

Much smaller than room 504B. No wonder Felix had been so attached to that room.

Ralph, Bernard and I could barely all stand in the room at the same time. And lined up on the wall were not one, not two, but **THREE** beds.

'A triple bunk bed?' said Ralph, sounding horrified.

'I don't even get my own side of the room?'

'Why aren't there any windows in here?' said
Bernard, tugging on his collar. Bernard doesn't
like small spaces. I suddenly wondered if that
was going to be a bit of an issue at Space Camp.

'There's a window right there,' I said
reassuringly, pointing up at the ceiling where
there was a small circular window.

'That isn't a window to the actual outside,'

said Bernard. 'That's a window to inside the space station.'

'Calm down, would you?' said Ralph. 'Watch.' He climbed up on the top bunk bed, and stood so he could reach the window in the ceiling. He twisted a big silver handle below it, and with a huff, pushed the window open. 'Just pretend that it is really the night sky.'

Bernard took a few deep breaths. 'Thanks, Ralph,' he said. 'That actually really helps.'

'How did you know how to open the window?' I asked. 'I'm surprised it opened actually. You definitely should **NOT** open windows on a spaceship in outer space.'

Ralph pointed at the silver handle. 'It was obvious,' he said. Then he looked down at us from the top bunk. 'If I have to sleep in a bunk bed, I'm claiming the top bunk.'

That was fine with me. I don't always love heights. Of course

I'm not **SCARED** of heights,

I just choose to avoid them if I can.

'I can't be in the middle,' said Bernard quickly. 'It's too crammed in here already.' He looked at me. 'Sam, is it okay if I take the bottom bunk?'

'No problem,' I said. 'I'll take the middle bunk.' I didn't say that the middle bunk was both too high for my liking AND too crammed, because sometimes being a good friend means letting your friends have the nicer things.

The loudspeaker in the corner crackled.

'*All space cadets please report to the canteen. REPEAT: all space cadets please report to the canteen.*'

I grinned at Ralph and Bernard. 'Time for our first space meal!'

CHAPTER 6

THE BEST WAY TO STAKE YOUR CLAIM

Luckily, we found the canteen without any issues.

There were four tables, each one a different colour. Zoe and Regina spotted us and waved us over. They were already sitting at the blue table.

Sally was nowhere to be found.

'Guess what,' said Zoe as soon as we sat down.

'What?' I said.

'Sally is in our room! And she took the top bunk without even asking! Everybody knows that is the best bunk,' Zoe said.

'That's why I took it,' said Ralph, looking smug.

'I thought we'd play rock-paper-scissors for it or something,' Zoe went on. 'But she just zoomed up the ladder and then she **SPAT** on her pillow to claim it!'

Regina wrinkled her nose. 'It's true, she really did do that.'

'And then she refused to leave the room for lunch,' Zoe said. 'So we just left her there.'

'I promised her I'd bring her back some food,' added Regina.

'Well,' I said, trying really hard to find a positive, 'sounds like she's good at climbing. That might come in handy in one of the challenges.'

'And spitting!' added Bernard.

'I'm good at climbing **AND** spitting,' said Zoe. 'We don't need her for that.'

It is true. Zoe can spit further than anyone I know. She learned how from her brother Toby. And she loves climbing trees and isn't even scared to jump off the high dive at the pool.

'We might need multiple spitters,' I said.

Just then, Commander Sharon walked over. She wasn't alone. She had her hands on Sally and was more or less marching her towards our table.

'We found one of your crew hiding out in her sleep pod,' Commander Sharon said cheerfully.

'I wasn't hiding,' said Sally, much less cheerfully. 'I just didn't want to come to lunch.'

'Can't have that attitude at Space Camp,' Commander Sharon said. 'Now, I know the rest of you know each other from school, so maybe make an extra effort so that Sally feels included.'

Sally glared at all of us. Grown-ups **never** know the right thing to say. You can't just tell someone to be friends and it magically makes them friends.

But still. Just being on a team together doesn't mean you have to be friends. I know that from **SPACE BLASTERS**. Sometimes **Spaceman Jack** and **Captain Jane** have to work together with all kinds of different creatures and aliens that they don't get along with. As **Spaceman Jack** says, sometimes, for the good of the universe, you have to put your differences aside.

'Can I count on you?' said Commander Sharon, looking right at me.

I saluted her. **'Yes, Commander!'** I said, louder than I meant to.

'Wonderful,' said Commander Sharon. She steered Sally to a chair next to me. 'I'll leave your crew to continue to get to know each other.' Then she leaned forwards and lowered her voice to a whisper. 'And I'll tell you a **SECRET**.

The very first Space Camp challenge is about
to start!'

My mouth dropped open. We weren't
ready for any challenges yet! One of our crew
members didn't want to be here! Bernard hadn't

had a chance to do any research! Ralph was still being, well, Ralph! We were **VERY** unprepared.

All my worries must have shown on my face because Regina patted my arm. 'It's okay, Sam,' she said. 'We'll be fine.'

'Yeah!' added Bernard. 'We're going to be great!'

I nodded. They were right. Everything was going to be great.

CHAPTER 7

SPACE FOOD EXPLOSION

I was really glad it was lunchtime. I hadn't had anything to eat since breakfast at home, which seemed like **A MILLION YEARS AGO**.

'I wonder what we'll get for lunch,' I said. I suddenly noticed there weren't any forks and knives on the table. Or plates.

'Well, what do they eat in space?' said Regina.

Bernard scrunched his face up. 'Sam, didn't you say once that they eat food from **TUBES** in space? Like spaghetti and meatballs blended up and put in a tube?'

'Like baby food?' asked Zoe.

'There is no way I'm eating food from a tube,' said Ralph.

It hadn't occurred to me that we might be getting **REAL** space food!

'Good afternoon, everyone!' said Commander Margaret from the back. 'I'm hearing lots of chit-chat about what we might be having for lunch.' She held up a green tube that looked like a tube of paint. 'Well, this is your first course!'

 Ralph turned the same shade of green as the tube.

'I'm not telling you what it is. Or what your second course is either.' She held up another tube. That one was orange. 'Or your third!' She held up one that was a kind of greyish white. 'Or any of them! For your first challenge, we want you to see if you can tell what kind of food is in each tube.'

'Space food is getting more and more advanced,' added Commander Wes, 'but food tubes with the right amount of nutrients are still one of the best ways to make sure that astronauts get everything they need. And in a convenient on-the-go package!'

'Not wasting food is also very important in space. Everything is perfectly measured out for the estimated length of the mission,' said Commander Sharon.

'Although one time, pizza was delivered to the International Space Station – the pizza was sent up onboard a resupply rocket.'[1]

We all laughed, imagining **PIZZA** going up to space!

'But for the challenge today, everything is in space food tubes. Each team will get a full meal, and the team who correctly identifies

the most ingredients, and finishes their space meals, wins,' said Commander Margaret.

My stomach growled again. I was hungry enough that even space food in a tube sounded good.

One of the Space Camp staff handed out six tubes to each of the tables and a sheet of paper to write down our answers. Three tubes were brightly coloured – orange, yellow and green. But the other three were indistinct mush colours – grey, white and a kind of sludge brown.

We stared at the tubes. I decided to take charge. It's what **Spaceman Jack** would do, after all.

'Who wants what colour?' I said.

'This is gross,' said Ralph. 'I don't want to eat anything that comes from a tube.'

'Ralph! Stop being such a brat about it,'

said Regina. ' And you've had food from a tube. Ketchup comes from a tube. And you love ketchup.' As Ralph's twin sister, she was the only one who knew how to put Ralph in his place.

'On my hot dogs! I don't want to eat an **ENTIRE TUBE** of ketchup,' Ralph said, but he grudgingly reached out and took the yellow tube. 'I'll try this one. It looks the most normal.'

Zoe took green, and Regina took orange.

That left me, Bernard and Sally with the mush-coloured ones.

'Maybe this one is chocolate,' Bernard said hopefully, taking the brownish one.

'You'd better hope it is chocolate,' said Ralph, eyeing it suspiciously.

I turned to Sally and held out the grey and the white tubes. 'Which one do you want?'

'I'm not eating **ANY** of that,' she said,

holding her nose. 'Ew.'

'But that's the challenge!' I said, trying not to get frustrated.

'Who cares?' she said, crossing her arms.

'**I CARE!**' I shouted. The team next to us looked over and I quickly sat down. 'I mean, it would be nice if you just tried it,' I said in my normal voice.

'Does everyone have their space food tubes?' said Commander Margaret from the front. 'Each team must write down what they think the foods are. When you are confident you have them right and have finished the tubes, the whole team must raise their hands. The first team to correctly identify all the foods wins. Remember, this is only the first challenge, but every point counts. Are there any questions?'

I had about a **MILLION** questions, but everyone else in the canteen was shaking their head, so I shook my head too.

'On the count of three we'll begin – one, two . . . three!'

Bernard squirted almost half the contents of his tube into his mouth before I'd even opened mine.

'Definitely not chocolate!' he said, brown coating his lips. He smacked his lips. 'Beans! It's black beans!'

'Are you sure?' I asked.

'Positive,' he said. He took another slurp. 'Not bad either.'

I squeezed my tube into my mouth. It was strangely familiar . . .

And then it hit me. It tasted like the fish balls Na-Na makes and puts in noodle soup! '**FISH!** I've got fish!' I said.

'Ugh, I'm glad you got that one and not me,' said Ralph, who still hadn't opened his yellow tube.

'You have to try your tube!' I said. Ralph slowly unscrewed the top.

'Mine's sweet potato!' said Regina.

'I think I have broccoli,' said Zoe, hesitantly squirting the green tube into her mouth. She made a face. 'Yep, definitely broccoli.'

'**WE'RE ON A ROLL!**' I said, hopping up and down with excitement as I wrote down all our answers. 'Ralph?'

'Corn,' he said.

'Are you sure?' I asked.

'Of course I'm sure!' he said. 'I told you, I'm always sure.'

'Yeah, but the last time you said that you led us into Felix's room,' said Bernard, who was finishing off his tube of black beans. He had it

69

smeared all over his face.

'Well, this time I'm **EXTRA** sure,' said Ralph.

'We've almost got it!' I said. 'Sally?'

Sally's white tube lay untouched in front of her on the table.

'Come on, Sally,' I said. 'You have to try it!'

'I don't have to do anything!' she said, but she unscrewed the top of her tube.

'You can do it!' I said, in what I hoped was an encouraging manner.

Sally stared directly at me and slowly pointed the tube in the same direction.

Time seemed to go in slow motion.

'**NOOO!**' I shouted as she squeezed the entire tube of white goop out at me, hitting me straight in the face.

'Team Blue!' shouted Commander Wes. 'What is going on?'

'**CHICKEN!**' I shouted, because some of it had got in my mouth. 'It's definitely chicken! Quick, someone write it down!'

'Team Blue is disqualified for wasting food,' said Commander Wes. 'It is imperative that food is not wasted on a spaceship.'

'**NO!**' shouted everyone on our team except Sally, who looked infuriatingly pleased with herself.

'But we had all the right answers!' I said, wiping chicken goop out of my eyebrow.

'You need to get cleaned up, cadet,' said Commander Margaret. 'And you –' she looked at Sally – 'you are coming with me.'

'This is what happens when you let little kids come to Space Camp,' said Felix snootily from his table. 'Commander Wes, we've got all the right answers. And we didn't start a food fight.'

Commander Wes reviewed the answers from Felix's team and nodded. 'Team Red wins the Space Food Challenge!' he announced.

I felt something rising up in my chest and throat, all the way up to my eyes. I wouldn't cry. I wouldn't.

I blinked as fast as I could.

'Got some chicken in my eye,' I muttered. 'Bernard, could you pass me a napkin?'

'You've got it, Captain Sam,' said Bernard.

'You are still a great captain,' whispered Regina. 'It isn't your fault Sally decided to stage a mutiny!'

'I can't believe she squeezed the whole tube on you,' said Ralph, sounding a little bit impressed.

'We've still got three more challenges,' said Zoe. 'We can still be Space Camp champions!'

Even though I was covered in tube chicken goop, I smiled at my friends. They were right. We couldn't give up now! As **Spaceman Jack** always says, ***when things get tough, the only option is to get tougher.***

I decided I wasn't going to let Sally ruin Space Camp.

But little did I know, she was about to be the least of my worries.

CHAPTER 8

EMERGENCY DEBRIEF

'We need a plan to deal with Sally.'

It was after the failed lunch challenge and I had called a team meeting in our sleep pod room. We were all crammed in. Bernard, Regina, Zoe and I sat on the floor, and Ralph was lying on his stomach on his top bunk, looking down at all of us. I couldn't believe that somehow, after finally befriending my long-term nemesis, Ralph, I now had to deal with a new, even worse nemesis.

Sally Doyle.

'Was she in your sleep pod?' I continued, looking at Zoe and Regina.

They shook their heads. 'I think she was taken to some sort of time-out or detention.'

'Good,' I said. 'I hope she stays in there. Then she can't sabotage our missions!' I tried to ignore the feeling of having been a little bit mean.

'She has proven to be quite the saboteur,' said Bernard. 'I'm not sure how we are ever going to get her to cooperate in our missions.'

'What even is a **SABOTEUR?**' asked Ralph with a snort.

'Someone who sabotages – ruins – a successful mission on purpose!' said Bernard, smiling at me. 'I learned that on SPACE BLASTERS.'

'Okay then, smarty-pants,' said Ralph with a sneer, 'what do they do with saboteurs on

SPACE BLASTERS?'

'Well, usually the SPACE BLASTERS crew outsmart the saboteurs and banish them to a distant planet,' I said. 'But I don't think we can do that to Sally.'

The door to our room swung open.

'What can't you do to me?' Sally demanded, her hands on her hips. 'I could hear you space losers jabbering from all the way down the hallway.'

This was **NOT** how to deal with a saboteur.

'Where have you been?' I said, resisting the urge to step back just in case Sally decided to squirt something at me again.

'I was put in *space jail*,' she said. 'And it was my last warning. Now I have to play nice or I get kicked out of Space Camp.'

'You don't really seem like you want to be here,' Regina said. 'So why would getting kicked out be so bad?'

Sally sighed dramatically and leaned against the doorway. 'Because this is the sixth camp I've been to in the past year, and if I get kicked out of another one I'm pretty sure my parents will ship me off to Antarctica.'

'I'd quite like to go to Antarctica,' said Bernard.

'Not the point, Bernard,' said Zoe. She looked at Sally. 'If you're going to be on our team, you have to **REALLY** be on our team. No more sabotaging, okay?'

'Ugh, you guys are so boring,' said Sally. 'But fine. I'll be a team player.' She put her hands up in quotes when she said **'TEAM PLAYER'**.

'Not that our team has a chance of winning.'

'You might not realize it,' I said, 'but we're an excellent team. Very brave. We can handle **ANYTHING**. Last Halloween, we took on zombies.'

'And won!' added Regina.

'And before that,' I said, warming to my theme, 'we hunted ghosts!'

As I said the word 'ghosts', the lights flickered off and on, and there was a loud **SLAM** from above us.

We all jumped, even Sally. Ralph was so startled, he hit his head on the ceiling above his bunk.

'Ow!' he said, rubbing his head. Then he frowned. 'What made the window slam shut?' he asked, pointing at the circular window that he'd opened earlier.

'Maybe a gust of wind?' Zoe suggested.

'But we're **indoors**,' said Bernard, starting to look anxious.

'Well, maybe it was the air con, or something.'

'Did you guys notice that the lights went out and the window slammed **RIGHT** as I said the word "ghosts"?' I said. The hairs on the back of my neck were standing up and I had goosebumps all over me.

'For a group that claims to be sooo brave, you all seem pretty scared of a little bit of flickering light,' said Sally, but even she looked a little shaken.

'That was no normal flickering light,' I said with as much authority as I could muster. 'That was the **GHOST KING**.'

CHAPTER 9

GHOSTS DON'T WEAR SOCKS

'Who is the Ghost King?' asked Sally, folding her arms and leaning back against the door. Even though she was trying to look cool, I could tell she was worried. As she should have been. **ANYONE** should be worried about the Ghost King.

'Just the scariest thing in the entire universe,' I said, keeping my voice steady. 'You'd better hope it isn't the Ghost King.'

'How are we going to focus on the Space Camp challenges if we're worried about the Ghost King?' asked Regina.

'We can **rise to the occasion**,' I said grandly. This is a phrase that **Spaceman Jack** says a lot on **SPACE BLASTERS** when they have to do something hard or that they don't want to do.

Everyone nodded. Even Sally.

Later that night, after we'd had a normal dinner in the canteen of chicken nuggets and **NOT** space food in tubes, Bernard, Ralph and I lay in our bunks.

'You two had better not snore,' said Ralph from his top bunk.

'I don't know if I snore,' said Bernard from the bottom bunk.

'You do,' I said from my middle bunk.

'I was worried I might,' said Bernard.

'Well, try not to,' said Ralph. 'At least you are the furthest away from me so hopefully I won't hear you.'

'I'll try,' said Bernard. 'Goodnight,' he added.

'Goodnight,' I said.

'Don't snore,' said Ralph.

We were quiet for a moment, and I thought they had fallen asleep.

'Hey, Sam,' whispered Bernard from the bunk below me.

'Yeah?' I whispered back.

'This is going to be the longest I've ever been

away from home,' he said.

'Me too,' I said. I hadn't realized it till right that very second and all of a sudden I missed my bed and my room and my parents and my sister and Na-Na and even Fang and Butterbutt **A LOT**.

'You're glad we came to Space Camp, right?' said Bernard. 'Even though we're away from home? And the Ghost King is probably on the loose?'

'If he is on the loose, we're the best people to deal with it,' I said, hoping I sounded more confident than I felt. 'Other than **Spaceman Jack** and **Captain Jane**,' I added.

'Hey, Sam,' Bernard said again.

'Yeah?'

'I'm glad I'm at Space Camp with you.'

I smiled in the dark.

'Me too,' I said.

'Will you two go to sleep?' said Ralph with a huff from up in his bunk. Then he paused. 'You guys are glad I'm here too, right?'

I smiled wider. 'Yeah, I am,' I said.

And the funny thing was, I meant it.

☆ 🚀 ☆

It was weird not seeing daylight the next morning.

'I miss the sun,' Bernard said, looking out of the window at the pretend night sky while we had breakfast in the canteen.

'We can't go too close to the sun in space,' I said. 'We'd get burnt to a crisp.'

'I don't think I'd do very well in space,' Bernard admitted. 'I'd miss Earth too much.'

'I'd be great, obviously,' said Ralph, chomping down on a piece of toast.

Just then, Zoe, Regina and Sally ran in. They all looked **EXTREMELY** serious.

'What's wrong?' I said when they reached our table, because something was clearly not right.

'We each had something go missing in the night!' said Zoe. 'This morning, I couldn't find my lucky purple socks. And then Regina couldn't find her favourite blue headband.'

'And my bracelet is missing,' said Sally.

'I don't get what the **BIG DEAL** is,' said Ralph. 'Regina, you lose your headbands all the time. Maybe you forgot to pack the blue one.'

Regina shook her head so fast that her hair whipped Zoe and Sally in the face. 'I definitely packed it. And last night I put it on top of my shelf so I wouldn't have to look for it this morning. But when I woke up, it was gone.'

'And I wanted my lucky purple socks for the challenge today. I always wear them on race days and then I win,' said Zoe.

'Who would want a pair of stinky purple socks?' said Ralph.

'I know who,' I said grimly. I looked up at Bernard and Zoe. 'Are you two thinking what I'm thinking?'

'I don't know,' said Bernard. 'What are you thinking?'

'This looks like the work of . . .' I paused, 'the Ghost King.'

This did **NOT** have the reaction I was expecting.

'What would the Ghost King want with my socks?' said Zoe. 'Ghosts don't even have feet. Not even the Ghost King.'

'It isn't about wearing socks,' I said. 'It's about causing **HAVOC!** Don't you remember the last episode of **SPACE BLASTERS** that we watched? Things on the ship started going **MISSING!** And because nobody could have got on or off the ship they knew it had to be the Ghost King. This is the **EXACT SAME SITUATION**.'

Ralph snorted. 'I wouldn't say it is exactly the same,' he said. 'First of all, we aren't on a locked ship, and, most importantly, we're not on a TV show.'

I just shook my head. 'Ralph, on the subject of ghosts, I definitely know what I'm talking about. **ESPECIALLY** if we're talking about the Ghost King.'

'Sam's right,' said Regina. 'He knows more about this kind of thing than we do. I hadn't even thought that it might be the Ghost King.'

'We're going to have to be on **VERY** high alert,' I said and then I looked at Sally. 'You're lucky you ended up on our team. We're ghost experts. We'll get your bracelet back.'

'Thanks,' she said, sounding the nicest she'd been since we met her. Then her eyes widened. 'Have you guys checked to see if anything is missing in **YOUR** room? I bet the Ghost King went in there too!'

Bernard and I looked at each other in a panic. 'You're right!' I said. 'We didn't check to see if anything was missing before we left the room this morning!'

'A huge oversight,' said Bernard.

'Why would we check to see if anything had vanished from a room we'd been in all night?' said Ralph with a scoff. 'You are all overreacting.'

'Ralph, didn't you hear Sam?' said Regina. 'The Ghost King could have gone into your room without you even noticing! Ghosts can float through walls. **AND** they are invisible.'

'I'm impressed with your ghost knowledge,' I said. Regina smiled at me.

'Fine,' said Ralph, throwing his hands up. 'We'll go and look to see if anything in our room is missing. But there won't be. You three just misplaced some things.'

'All three of us? At the **SAME TIME**?'

said Regina. 'How likely is that?'

'More likely than a ghost coming in and stealing stuff,' said Ralph.

'It isn't just the missing stuff,' I said. 'Remember the lights flickering last night? And the window slamming shut? All **very** clear signs of the Ghost King.'

'I guess you *do* know more about this stuff than me,' Ralph admitted.

I was so surprised, I almost fell off my chair. Ralph never admits knowing less than anybody. **EVER**. 'Let's go back to our room,' I said.

It didn't take us long to discover what was missing.

'My watch is missing!' said Ralph.

'My grandpa gave it to me!'

'And my green pen!' said Bernard, frantically digging around in his backpack. 'It's my favourite pen! I got it when I was on holiday with my dad.'

'Guys, mine is the worst of all,' I said. I paused to let that sink in. 'The Ghost King stole my can of poison mist'.[1]

---

[1] Technically my mum's hairspray, but have you ever walked into a cloud of hairspray and NOT coughed? Totally poison mist. Perfect for fighting ghosts.

CHAPTER 10

THE SPACE CHAIR

'This is a **SITUATION**,' I said. 'We have to stay **CALM**.'

'Sam, you are the least calm of all of us,' said Ralph.

We were back with the rest of Team Blue in the main area, getting ready for our next challenge.

'I just can't believe the Ghost King took my poison mist,' I said, shaking my head. 'It's as if he knew what was most important to all of us.'

'You brought . . . poison mist to Space Camp?' said Sally, staring at me wide-eyed. 'They let you bring that in?'

97

'It's hairspray. He brought his mum's hairspray. He claims it is poison mist,' said Ralph.

'Don't you remember the time I accidentally sprayed you with it?' I said. 'You were **TOTALLY** incapacitated for at **LEAST** a minute. Do not underestimate the power of poison mist.'

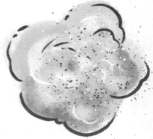

'Well, it doesn't matter how powerful this so-called poison mist is now, because the Ghost King has stolen it,' said Sally.

'Oh no!' said Regina, covering her mouth with her hands. 'What if he is planning to use the poison mist **ON US?**'

'Luckily, we'll survive,' said Ralph. 'As it is just hairspray. Is nobody listening to me?'

'There is definitely a ghost on this ship,' I said, scanning the area all around me. 'And we're the only ones who can catch it.'

'Attention, everyone!' said Commander Margaret from the front. 'It's time for your next challenge. Today you will be experiencing the Five

Degrees of Freedom simulator. Or, as I like to

call it, the **SPACE CHAIR**.'

'Let's worry about the Ghost King after

this challenge,' I whispered. Then I stared hard

at Sally. 'You'd better not try to sabotage us

again. We have enough to worry about!'

She held up her hands. 'Don't worry about

me,' she said. 'I'm glad I'm on your team now.

With the ghost and everything.'

'Team Blue,' said Commander Margaret,

'please be quiet. I don't want you to miss any of

the instructions.'

'Or to be disqualified, **AGAIN**,' said Felix

with a nasty laugh.

'Sorry, Commander!' I said. I ignored Felix. But

I saw Sally glare at him.

'As I was saying,' said Commander Margaret,

'the Space Chair simulates the kind of movement that astronauts would have onboard their ships and even what they feel when tethered to the ship outside to make repairs to it. Of course, here at Space Camp we are still subject to the laws of gravity, but this will give you a good idea of what it would feel like.'

'Now,' said Commander Sharon, stepping forwards. 'I have some serious news for everyone. Last night, a small asteroid hit the side of our ship,' she said.

I gasped.

'Calm down, Sam. It's not a real asteroid,' said Ralph, shaking his head. 'It's obviously just part of the challenge.'

'If I may continue,' said Commander Sharon, 'a small asteroid hit the side of our ship. We need to repair it, and the only way to do that is to go outside the ship in the Space Chair.'

'Each team will be in a relay race to see who can move most quickly across the ship in the Space Chair to repair the damage,' said Commander Wes, passing out coloured ropes to each team. 'You'll have to work together to figure out where to go next.'

'Is everyone ready to go out into space?' said Commander Margaret.

We all cheered.

'Then let's go.'

The Space Camp commanders led us to a giant wall with crisscrossing metal bars all over it, like scaffolding. Attached to the scaffolding were four chairs. A member of each team had to sit in the chair and then, using ropes and pulleys, scramble across the wall and tie their

ribbons to different points, before the next member of their team took a turn in the chair.

Bernard stared up at the wall with a focused expression on his face. I knew that look. It was his thinking-hard look.

'What do you think, Bernard?' I said.

'I'm just doing some calculations in my head,' he said, and the tip of his tongue stuck out of the side of his mouth, so I knew he was **REALLY** focused.

'I've got a plan,' he said. He motioned to the rest of our team. 'Listen to me.'

I sat back and let Bernard explain the maths he'd done (in his head!) and how we should climb the wall in the Space Chair. Part of being a good captain is knowing when to let others take the lead, and this was definitely one of those times.

The order we went in was **VERY** important.

Zoe, as the fastest and most athletic member of our team, had to go last. Bernard was going to go first, because then he could spend the rest of the time directing the others where to go. I also suspected this was because Bernard did **NOT** love heights, and by going first he was able to stay closest to the ground.

'Okay, everyone got it?' said Bernard, looking at each of us. I felt strangely proud of him. He was in his element.[1] It's nice when your friends are good at something and you can cheer them on.

We all nodded. I stared at Sally. 'Even you?' Bernard had put her third, so if there was any funny business it wouldn't slow us down at the start or at the end.

---

[1] This means seeing someone really enjoying something they are good at.

Sally gave me a tight smile and put her thumbs up. I figured it was the most enthusiasm we were going to get out of her.

I grinned at my team. '**For the universe!**'[2] I said, shooting my hand up in the air with my finger pointed upwards like a rocket.

'**For the universe!**' shouted my team. Well, almost my whole team. Sally just rolled her eyes. Even Ralph said it, although a little bit quieter than the rest of us. But it didn't matter. We had the best team and I **KNEW** it.

Then it was time for the challenge.

'On your marks, get set, **GO!**' said Commander Wes.

---

[2] This is the **SPACE BLASTERS** motto. I like to use it as much as I can.

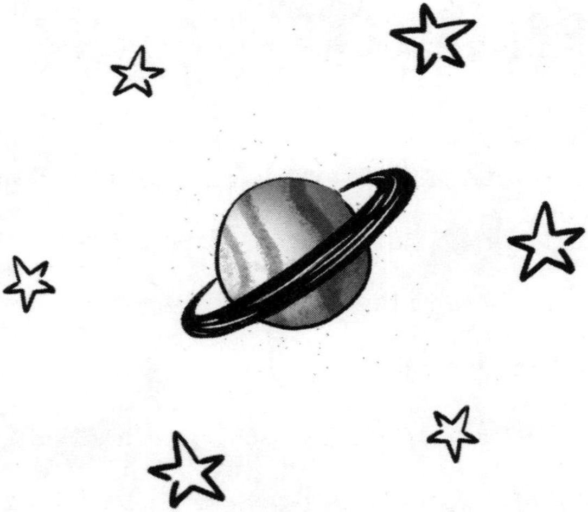

CHAPTER 11

REAL ROCKET SCIENCE

Bernard scuttled like a beetle along the wall, left, then right, then sideways, and then triumphantly tied his blue ribbon on the designated corner.

He came back to Earth, quickly unbuckled his seat belt and hopped out of the chair. All around us teams were cheering and each time a member of a team completed their leg, a bell rang.

It was my turn next.

I'd never felt so much like an astronaut as I did when Commander Margaret secured my seat belt in the Space Chair.

'Ready, Sam?' she said with a smile.

'Ready!' I said, and then I held my breath as I was spun towards the wall.

'Sam, go diagonally up and then tie the ribbon in the far corner,' shouted Bernard.

The chair moved smoothly as I glided from one direction to the next. It was the closest feeling I'd ever had to being able to fly. And for the first time ever, I wasn't even a little bit nervous about heights because I felt so secure in the Space Chair. It was **AMAZING**.

If we hadn't been in a race, I would have stayed in the Space Chair, going from one side of the wall to the other, for as long as I could. But it was a race, and I wanted my team to win, so as soon as I tied my ribbon to the wall, I lowered myself back to Earth.

'Good job, Sam!' said Zoe, giving me a high five.

'Yeah, you were great!' said Regina. 'We're winning! The other teams are only just sending their second team members up.'

'It's all thanks to Bernard,' I said, grinning at Bernard. 'He's the brains of the operation.' That's what **Spaceman Jack** always says about **Captain Jane**.

'It isn't actual rocket science,' said Sally as she was strapped into the Space Chair. 'It's just a silly competition.'

'Actually,' said Commander Sharon, 'the problem-solving you have to do for this challenge is related to real rocket science, which is why we're getting you to do it.'

'Whatever,' sighed Sally.

'Sally,' I said, 'don't forget, you **PROMISED** no sabotaging!'

'Yeah, yeah,' she said, spinning around to face the wall. 'Don't worry, I'll do the stupid challenge. But I didn't promise I wouldn't make fun of you space nerds.'

'Why is she even here?' moaned Bernard.

As I watched Sally go up in the Space Chair, my palms started to sweat. She couldn't let us down again, it just wouldn't be fair!

And then, to our surprise, she kept her promise. She flew up and across the crisscrossing bars of the wall, almost as if she'd done it before.

'Wow,' said Bernard. 'That's pretty impressive.'

FOR THE UNIVERSE!

After Sally, it was Regina's turn. 'You guys can count on me,' she said with a for-the-universe salute and up she went.

I realized that Ralph had been surprisingly quiet all this time. I turned to him. 'Ralph, everything okay?'

He was biting one of his nails. 'Everything is fine, just fine,' he said. 'Why wouldn't it be? Mind your own business, Sam!'

'You're on my team,' I said. 'And you're up next! Your business is my business!' I frowned. 'You aren't afraid of heights, are you? You're in the top bunk!'

'Of course I'm not afraid of heights,' Ralph said with one of his signature snorts.

But I could **TELL** something was bothering him.

'Well, what is it then?'

Ralph glared at me for a second. Then he kind of deflated, like a balloon that'd had all the air taken out of it.

115

'It isn't the heights. I hate team projects. What if I mess it up?'

I stared at him. I'd never heard Ralph even come close to admitting that **ANYTHING** made him nervous.

I'd never thought the time would come when RALPH PHILIP ZINKERMAN THE THIRD, my former nemesis, would need a pep talk from me, SAM WU *(previously known to Ralph as Scaredy-Cat Sam)*.

But the time was here. And luckily, thanks to one of my favourite episodes of SPACE BLASTERS when **Spaceman Jack** thinks he should start flying his own ship and **Captain Jane** has to convince him to stay and be part of the SPACE BLASTERS crew, I knew just what to say.

'Ralph,' I said, 'the best part of being on a team is that everyone else is here for you. You can't let us down. No matter what.' Then I patted him on the back.

'Okay,' he said, but he didn't sound as convinced or as confident as **Spaceman Jack** did.

'Your turn, Ralph,' said Commander Sharon as Regina was unhooked from the Space Chair.

And up Ralph went.

'You can do it, Ralph!' I yelled.

And then something awful occurred to me.

Ralph's hands were empty. He'd forgotten the ribbon to tie on.

'Ralph! Come back down!' I yelled.

'What?' he shouted back.

'What are you talking about, Sam?' said Bernard.

I held up the blue ribbon Ralph had left

on the floor. 'Ralph forgot his ribbon!' I waved it in the air.

As Ralph realized what I was holding, first his eyes widened and then he scrunched his face up. For a moment, I thought he was going to cry.

'Don't worry, Ralph!' I yelled. 'Just come back down!'

We were still ahead, but the others were gaining on us.

'Here! Give me the ribbon!' said Zoe, grabbing it out of my hands. Before Ralph was even back on Earth, she had pushed it into his hands. '**Keep going!**' she said. Ralph went back up with the ribbon as fast as he could, but it wasn't fast enough. Team Red, with Felix, had taken the lead.

'I'm sorry,' said Ralph as he arrived back and Commander Sharon unstrapped him from the

Space Chair. He wouldn't look at any of us. 'I've lost it for us.'

'One of us should have checked for your ribbon,' I said. 'Don't beat yourself up!'

'Yeah, don't say that!' said Regina. 'We've still got one leg to go!'

'And it's **MY** turn,' said Zoe with a wide smile as she jumped into the Space Chair to get strapped in. 'There's a reason we saved me for last!'

Ralph smiled gratefully.

'You'd better be fast,' urged Bernard, eyeing the wall. 'Felix is already on the wall!'

'I'm always fast,' said Zoe as Commander Sharon secured the last strap of the Space Chair.

And then she kicked off and shot up to the top of the scaffolding.

'GO, ZOE!'

we screamed from Earth. I was jumping up and down and my voice was getting hoarse from so much yelling.

Zoe passed Felix in a blur of arms and legs, and then she stretched up and secured the final ribbon to the corner of our section.

'And Team BLUE have repaired the damage on their side of the ship first!' announced Commander Wes.

We all started jumping up and down and hugging each other – even Sally!

It was the best feeling I'd ever had.

CHAPTER 12

TAKE A SPIN IN SPACE

We were so excited by our big win on the Space Chair, we all forgot about the threat of the Ghost King for a little bit. But not for long.

The next day it was time for the activity I was **MOST** looking forward to. But also the one that I was just a **LITTLE** bit nervous about.

Going for a spin in the Multi-Axis Trainer.

It's a machine that **REAL** astronauts use to prepare for going up into space. It is made of three interlocking rings and the astronaut is strapped in the middle – almost like going inside a giant hamster wheel that spins in every possible direction. It helps prepare the astronauts to be in zero gravity and how to orientate themselves no matter what direction they're flying in.

'Now,' said Commander Margaret, 'I'd like to remind you all that this isn't one of the challenges. We just want each of you to have a chance to experience the Multi-Axis Trainer, just like real astronauts. Everyone will have a turn.'

'Commander Margaret,' said Commander Wes, 'don't you mean that everyone will have several turns?' He laughed at his own joke.

Felix laughed too, as if it was the funniest thing he'd ever heard. He was obviously trying to suck up to Commander Wes.

'He's the worst,' said Ralph, glowering at Felix.

I had to agree with Ralph there.

There were four Multi-Axis Trainers, so each team had to decide who would go first. Because Zoe had won us the challenge yesterday, everyone agreed she should get to go first.

'And I'll go last,' I said.

'Is it because you're scared?' said Ralph. And then I remembered why he had been my nemesis for so long. It was like he was **DELIBERATELY** forgetting how nice I'd been to him yesterday.

'No, it's because I'm being a good captain and letting my team experience it first,' I said.

'That's really nice of you, Sam,' said Regina.

'*I still think you're scared*,' grinned Ralph said with a grin.

'I'm **NOT** scared,'

I said. And I wasn't. At least I wasn't **VERY** scared. Although if I had known what was going to happen when I went on, I might have been a **LITTLE** bit more scared.

'This thing actually looks cool,' said Sally, staring at the giant interlocking circles.

'I'm worried I might throw up,' said Bernard.

'You won't throw up,' said Commander Wes.

'How do you know?'

'Same way I know anything else – science! Because your stomach remains centred, you won't feel nauseated. And because the Multi-Axis Trainer doesn't spin more than twice in a row in the same direction, your inner ear fluid doesn't shift, so you won't even get dizzy.'

Bernard nodded. Facts always reassure him.

I watched as one at a time my friends each took a turn on the Multi-Axis Trainer. There were even more seat belts on this one than on the Five Degrees of Freedom simulator (aka the Space Chair) because the Multi-Axis Trainer went upside down and spun all around. Each time someone went on it they looked super scared at the start and super excited at the end. I hoped it would be that way for me.

I couldn't decide if time was taking **FOREVER** while I waited or if it was going too fast, but I definitely didn't feel ready when it was my turn.

Even though Commander Wes had said that the Multi-Axis Trainer wouldn't make us throw up, my stomach was already jumping up and down inside me before I even got on it. The last thing I needed was another **INCIDENT**[1] on a space simulator.

I swallowed as hard as I could, trying to get my stomach to go back to where it belonged and out of my throat.

---

[1] All you need to know about THAT is that I went in the Astro Blast Simulator at the Space Museum and the Ghost King tried to get me and something VERY embarrassing happened. It involved a pair of wet pants and was the start of Ralph calling me Scaredy-Cat Sam. So this couldn't be the thing that defeated me!

The helmet felt extra tight on my head and my hands were so sweaty it was hard for me to hold on to the handles.

As Commander Wes strapped me in, I asked him to double-check all the buckles just in case. He laughed and said safety was always the first priority at Space Camp, but that he'd check just for me.

And then I was in. And it started spinning. And spinning. And I didn't know which way was up or which way was down and everything around me was a blur and it was

AWESOME.

'*Woohoo!*' I yelled, and I thought I heard my friends laughing, not **AT** me in a mean way, but **WITH** me in a happy way, but I was going fast I couldn't tell. I thought maybe I really **COULD** be an astronaut one day and then I thought about how proud **Spaceman Jack** and Captain Jane would be of me and then ...

DARKNESS.

TOTAL,

COMPLETE

DARKNESS.

CHAPTER 13

RETURN OF THE GHOST KING

Everyone started yelling.

AND I KEPT SPINNING.
IN TOTAL, COMPLETE
AND UTTER DARKNESS.

If I'd been confused about which direction I'd

been going in before, now I really had NO idea

where I was. It was like being tossed around in a

washing machine, but without the water.

GET ME OFF THIS THING! I

shouted. And then I closed my eyes, even

though it was dark, and tried to count to ten.

Captain Jane said once on **SPACE BLASTERS** –

when she was hung up by her ankles by evil aliens and being interrogated for top-secret information – that she could withstand anything for ten seconds. I could too. And I **DEFINITELY** could do it without peeing my pants.[1]

In that moment, I've never been so glad that I only had one glass of orange juice at breakfast.

I kept spinning. And spinning. And then a **SUPER LOUD** alarm sounded and the spinning stopped with a loud shriek and then all the lights came back on.

---

[1] This is related to the earlier INCIDENT I mentioned.

I was hanging
upside down.
But I was alive.

Just like **Captain Jane**,
I'd survived and lived to tell my tale.

'Get the kids out **NOW**!' shouted
Commander Margaret, looking more stressed
than I'd ever seen her.

'Sam! Are you okay?' said Bernard. He was
so pale he was almost green, as if **HE** were the
one who had been spun around a million times in
the dark.

I managed to nod. Or at least I tried to nod.
It's very hard to nod when you are stuck upside
down.

'Let's get you out of this thing,' said
Commander Wes, manually spinning the Multi-
Axis Trainer till I was right side up. It was the

first time I'd ever seen him look serious.

'What **HAPPENED**?' I asked Commander Wes as he unstrapped me.

'I'm not totally sure,' he admitted. 'Seems as if the power went out there for a second. But just on the lights. We'll have to check the wiring – that should never happen.'

I stumbled out of the Multi-Axis Trainer. My knees were wobbly and I almost fell. Luckily, Zoe and Bernard caught me.

'Whoa, careful, Sam!' said Zoe.

'Let him catch his breath,' said Regina.

'That was **WILD**,' said Ralph, staring at me with wide eyes. 'I'm glad it was you in there and not me.'

'Ralph!' said Regina, whacking her brother on the shoulder. 'Don't say that!'

'It's true!' said Ralph.

'I guess I'm just braver than you,' I said to Ralph.

All around us, the other kids who had been stuck spinning in darkness were helped out of the Multi-Axis Trainers. Everyone looked scared and stressed out.

'Space cadets!' shouted Commander Margaret from the front. 'Please stay in your teams and go directly to the canteen. We're going to give everyone some juice and cookies to help settle any upset stomachs and calm any nerves after what just happened. We've got staff looking into the lighting to make sure it won't happen again.'

As soon as my team and I sat down at our blue table, I burst out with my theory.

'That's confirmed it. It is most definitely the Ghost King! At Space Camp!'

Everyone stared at me with wide eyes. I could tell they were nervous and I didn't blame them.

'Are you sure?' asked Bernard, biting his nails.

'Look at the signs,' I said, listing them off on my fingers. 'Things going missing. Lights flickering on and off. Total **POWER OUTAGE** that even the Space Camp commanders can't explain. There's only ONE explanation.'

'And that explanation is a Ghost King?' said Sally, even more sceptically than Ralph. She also didn't look nervous AT ALL. It was definitely because she knew **NOTHING** about how serious the situation was.

'**THE** Ghost King, you mean,' I corrected. 'There is only one. And do **YOU** have any other ideas for what is going on here?'

For a second Sally looked as if she was going to say something else, but then she shook her head. 'Nope.'

'What are we going to do, Sam?' said Bernard. 'This is dangerous stuff.'

'Maybe we should tell the Space Camp commanders,' said Zoe.

'They won't believe us,' I said. I looked at Zoe and Bernard. 'Remember when we tried to tell my parents about the ghost in my house?'

They nodded solemnly.

'I guess you're right,' said Zoe.

'It's going to be up to us,' I said, looking

around at my crew. 'Everyone has to be on

CONSTANT VIGILANCE'.²

'Sam,' said Regina, 'I bet the Ghost King is working with alien ghosts. This must be part of a whole evil plan!'

'That's it!' I said. 'Why else would the Ghost King come to Space Camp?'

I lowered my voice. 'Just think of all the havoc the Ghost King could cause on a spaceship,' I said. 'On Earth, opening a door or a window is just a sign of a pesky ghost. On a spaceship . . .' I paused dramatically. Everyone just stared at me. I sighed. 'Obviously, if a door or window gets opened on a spaceship, you would get

---

² This means keeping an eye out for ANYTHING. Because the Ghost King could strike again at ANY moment.

sucked out into space and would pretty much die INSTANTLY because you wouldn't be able to breathe.'

'That's a very good point,' said Bernard, shuddering a little.

Even Sally was starting to look a little more anxious.

'Well, I'll remind you that we aren't technically IN space,' said Ralph. 'So we don't **ACTUALLY** need to worry about getting sucked out of any windows.'

'Lucky for us,' I said. 'But even if we aren't in **IMMINENT** danger of becoming space dust, I think we are all in agreement that the Ghost King, possibly with alien ghosts as accomplices, is here. Turning off lights, stealing things, causing all kinds of problems.'

Everyone nodded. Even Ralph and Sally.

'So what's the plan?' said Zoe.

'I don't think they have any pickle juice in the Space Camp kitchen, do you?' said Bernard. Last time we had a ghost issue we dealt with it by using a **WELL-KNOWN** ghost repellent – pickle juice[3].

<hr />

[3] Bernard learned about this on a very trustworthy sounding website, naturalghostremendies.org.

'All we can do is be alert,' I said. 'I think from now on, nobody should be alone. **EVER**.'

'What if we need to go to the bathroom?' said Sally.

'I'll wait outside the cubicle,' said Regina. 'Things are dire.'

'And you never know, the Ghost King might be hiding in a toilet,' I said. 'Even bathrooms aren't safe. **NOWHERE** is with the Ghost King on the loose and looking to cause trouble.'

'I've got to say, Sam,' said Ralph, 'I'd expect you to be more **SCARED** of the Ghost King.' I thought for a second he was making fun of me, but he was being serious.

'Well,' I said, 'this isn't my first time dealing with the Ghost King. And, as **Spaceman Jack** says, the more you face your fears, the less scary they become.'

That said, I **REALLY** hoped I wasn't going to have to actually come **FACE TO FACE** with the Ghost King in a toilet at Space Camp!

CHAPTER 14

ROCKET SABOTAGE

Even with **EVERYTHING** going on, Space Camp continued as normal. And after breakfast the next day, it was time for our next challenge – the rocket challenge. The Space Camp commanders said that they'd checked the lights and not to expect any other power outages.

'They definitely don't know what they are dealing with,' I whispered to my team as we went outside to make our rocket. We obviously couldn't shoot rockets off inside! So there was a special launch-pad area right outside the Space Camp building.

The sunlight felt extra bright after being inside for the past few days.

Space Camp staff passed out the materials for each team to make their own rocket.

'I've built and launched my own rockets before,' said Regina. 'I got a rocket kit last year for my birthday. Can I lead on this one?'

Definitely,' I said.

Regina picked up the hollow tube[1] and put the rocket engine inside. Then she carefully made the fins and attached them to the outside. Next she stuffed the parachute into the top of the tube. The last step was to put

---

[1] It kind of looked like an empty toilet paper roll.

the nose cone on top. She held it out for us to inspect. 'What do you guys think?'

Zoe whistled in admiration. 'That's **AWESOME**.'

'The question is, will it fly?' said Sally, eyeing the rocket.

'Of course it will fly!' said Ralph. 'Just look at it!'

'I think it should fly,' said Regina modestly. 'But I'm glad we get a chance to practise!'

'Let's go to the launch pad and test it out!' said Bernard.

'If we need to make any changes, we can do that on the final rocket.'

We went over to the launch pad, set up our test rocket in the designated area and then stood back as far as the fuse would let us.

'You should light it,' I said to Regina. 'Since you designed it.'

Regina lit the fuse and we all watched as the spark travelled fast until it was directly under the rocket. With a **BLAST**, our rocket took off and shot straight towards the sky.

'Wow!' I said, shading my eyes so I could follow the rocket's trajectory. Regina clapped her hands in delight. 'That's higher than any rocket I've ever made!'

We all gave her high fives as the rocket shot out a little parachute and came back down to Earth. Regina caught the rocket before it hit the ground.

'We're **DEFINITELY** going to win this one,' said Zoe.

'I don't even think it needs any improvements!' said Bernard. 'All we need to do is replace the internal motor and the fuse so we can use it again.'

We went back to our table and got our rocket ready for the real launch. The one that counted for points.

'I've got to say,' said a voice from behind us, 'that was pretty *good* for a bunch of pipsqueaks.' It was Felix.

We all turned to glare at him.

He held his hands up in mock surrender. 'What? I'm just trying to be nice. I can appreciate good engineering when I see it. Jeez, can't you guys take a compliment?'

'Not from the enemy,' said Zoe, hands on her hips.

'I actually came over here to say *good* luck, and may the best future astronaut win,' said Felix, holding his hand out for Zoe to shake. 'I wanted to shake hands with all of you.'

Zoe stared at his hand as if it were a snake.

'Oh come on,' said Felix with a frustrated sigh. 'I'm trying to show good sportsmanship here.'

'Okay, fine,' said Zoe, tentatively shaking

Felix's hand and then making a big show of wiping her hand off on her clothes afterwards.

Then Felix came around to all of us and shook our hands as if he were running for mayor or something. And **THEN** he did it a second time! We all shook his hand again because it seemed like the right thing to do. As **Spaceman Jack** says, there's no point in starting a space fight with someone who wants to be friends.

'Just to prove I really am rooting for you guys,' he said with a smile that showed all his teeth.

'Got it,' I said. 'Erm. Good luck to you too.'

'What's that funny little sign you guys do? Where you shoot your hand up?'

'For the universe?' I said, confused.

'Yeah, that's the one,' said Felix, and this time his smile was more of a smirk. I got a bad feeling in the pit of my stomach. 'For the universe,' he said and shot his fist up. But he did it wrong, because on **SPACE BLASTERS** they point a finger in the air too. It's more than a fist pump. But I didn't tell him that.

Felix was still grinning as he returned to his team.

'Well, that was weird,' I said to my team as we turned back to our rocket. I noticed something else weird then too. Sebastian, one of the people on Team Red, was walking away very quickly in the other direction. I knew that walk. It was a sneaky walk.

Something was definitely up.

'What is Sebastian up to?" said Sally, watching him go. 'That looks like a sneaky walk.'

'That's what I thought!' I said. "And didn't you think it was weird that Felix came over here?"

"You guys are reading into things way too much," said Regina. "I think Felix knows we're going to win and wants to be friends with the winning team.' Regina always thinks the best of everyone. Even people who **CLEARLY** are our enemies.

'Hmmm,' said Sally, staring after Felix. 'I don't know about that.'

We all went back out to the launch pad and lined up our rocket next to the other ones. I hated to admit it, but they all kind of looked the same. I knew our rocket was the best one though. Commander Margaret started the countdown. When she hit zero, we'd light the fuses. Regina stood, ready, with a match in hand.

'Five . . .'

Suddenly, I noticed something funny.

'Four...'

Regina had put a little SB for **SPACE BLASTERS** on our rocket fin.

'Three...'

And the rocket in front of us didn't have an SB on it.

'Two...'

In a panic I looked at the other rockets.

'One...'

And saw with horror that the rocket in front of Felix's Team Red had an SB on it.

Before I could say anything, the fuses were lit.

'Blast off!'

I couldn't bear to watch. I covered my face because I knew that our rocket was going to go the highest. And Team Red would get the credit for it.

'What's wrong with our rocket?' said Bernard. 'It's just . . . sputtering on the launch pad!'

'Why won't it take off?' said Zoe.

'I don't understand,' said Regina, her voice wobbling. 'It should fly just the way it did during the practice round!'

'Maybe when you replaced the motor you did it wrong,' said Sally, extremely unhelpfully.

I couldn't keep quiet. 'That isn't our rocket. They switched it! Look!' I pointed at Felix and Team Red. Up above them, OUR rocket was still going higher and higher into the sky.

'Looks as if we have a clear winner,' said Commander Margaret. 'Team Red wins!'

BUT THEY STOLE OUR ROCKET!

I shouted.

'What's that, Sam?' said Commander Wes, coming up behind us.

'Felix! He stole our rocket! He came over and pretended to be nice to us and then **STOLE OUR ROCKET**! And switched it with their terrible one! It didn't even take off!'

Everyone was staring at me now. I felt my face go hot with anger and embarrassment but I wasn't going to back down. Justice had to be served!

'Did you see him steal your rocket?' Commander Wes asked in an infuriatingly calm voice.

'Well, no,' I admitted. Because we hadn't. 'But I **KNOW** he did!'

The rocket started to come back down.

'Now, Sam,' said Commander Wes. 'I know that it isn't fun to lose and I know how hard your team worked on your rocket.'

'I can prove it,' I said. 'Regina painted an SB on our rocket, for **SPACE BLASTERS**, the best TV show in the universe, and THAT rocket –' I pointed at the one that had gone the highest and had just landed in front of Team Red – 'says SB on it.'

'Our rocket has SB on it because my name is Sebastian Burns,' said Sebastian. 'And I'm offended that you are not only implying that we are thieves, but that a bunch of kids could make a better rocket than us.'

'**YOU!**' I said, pointing at him.

IT WAS YOU!

'You saw Sebastian steal your rocket?' said Commander Wes in the same infuriatingly calm voice as before.

'No. But I saw him walking away! In a sneaky way!' I desperately looked around. 'Right, Sally?'

'It was one hundred per cent a sneaky walk,' said Sally. 'And I would know. Because I'm sneaky.'

'I don't know why you are bragging about being sneaky,' said Bernard, sounding baffled. 'But if you say it was a sneaky walk, it must have been.'

'I didn't see the sneaky walk, but I believe Sam,' said Zoe. 'And I know that was our rocket.' She crossed her arms.

'My sister would **NEVER** design a rocket that didn't fly,' said Ralph, looking angrier than I'd **EVER** seen him.

'This rocket doesn't even have an engine!' said

Regina, inspecting the rocket in front of us.

'Well, that isn't our fault,' said Felix. 'I'll admit you guys had a great rocket on your test run, but your engine must have fallen out or something when you brought it over to the launch pad.' He looked straight at me and gave me a nasty smile. 'Sorry, Sam. Looks like the best astronauts won, and it wasn't you guys.'

'Now there, Felix,' said Commander Wes, 'no need to rub it in. Team Blue are obviously very upset by the fact that their rocket didn't launch.'

'But our rocket **DID** launch,' I said again, but quieter this time. I felt defeated.

'And unfortunately, we're going to have to award Team Blue zero points for this challenge,' Commander Wes went on. 'Team Yellow came in third, Team Green came in second, and our winner is Team Red. Well done, everyone, even Team Blue. Excellent effort.'

'Sam,' said Bernard frantically, 'Sam, if we get zero points, it means there is **NO** way we can win the overall Space Camp competition!'

'There's nothing we can do now,' I said, hanging my head. 'Nobody believes us.' I looked up at Regina. 'We all know you made the best rocket, Regina,' I said.

Regina rubbed one of her eyes and I could tell she was trying not to cry. 'Thanks, Sam,' she said.

'It just isn't fair,' said Ralph. 'We should have won.'

I took a deep breath to calm myself. I knew it was up to me to reassure my team. 'We know we're the real winners,' I said. 'And nobody, not even stupid Felix and Team Red, can take that away from us.' I put my hand out in the middle.

'Is everyone with me?'

Regina gave me a small smile and put her hand out. 'I am,' she said.

'Me too,' said Zoe. 'We're definitely still the best team.'

'Team Blue forever!' said Bernard.

'At least it wasn't my fault this time,' said Sally, putting her hand in.

'All right, all right,' grumbled Ralph, 'I'll even say it.' He paused and looked at all of us. 'For the universe!'

'That's the spirit,' I said.

We might not have been the winning team, but we definitely were the best team.

It still would have been nice to win though.

CHAPTER 15

PERILS OF (ALMOST) ZERO GRAVITY

I think Felix and the rest of Team Red were surprised to see we were all still so cheerful.

'Morning, Sam,' Felix said in a really fake nice way as we walked past him at breakfast the next morning. 'How are you all feeling today?'

I scowled at him. 'We've got **MORE** important things to worry about than you.'

'And we know we made the best rocket,' added Zoe.

'Yeah!' said Bernard.

'How embarrassing for you that you had to

steal from younger kids,' said Regina.

'Pathetic, really,' said Ralph.

Felix started to turn a little red. 'I don't know what you're talking about,' he said. 'You are all just sore losers.'

'You keep telling yourself that,' said Sally with a smack of her gum.

'Team,' I said as we sat down at our table, 'I think we can all be very proud of how we've conducted ourselves. I know **Spaceman Jack** and **Captain Jane** would be proud of us.'

'You **REALLY** love that TV show, don't you?' said Sally.

'It's a pretty good show,' said Ralph.

I beamed.

'Good morning, space cadets!' said Commander Margaret. 'I'd like to remind everyone that the Space Camp competition is just for fun. We know everyone likes to win, but the important thing is that you are all enjoying yourselves and learning something!'

I sank down in my seat. I knew she was talking about our team.

I didn't even care that much about us not winning, but I hated that someone else had cheated. It just wasn't fair.

Felix was staring straight at our team with a smirk. I turned my head away. I wouldn't give him the satisfaction of knowing he had upset me.

There was no way I was going to let him ruin this activity too.

'Today, you'll be going on the one-sixth gravity chair. Now, does anyone know why the chair is set for one-sixth gravity?'

Bernard's hand flew up into the air.

'Yes, Bernard?' said Commander Margaret.

'Because the moon's gravitational pull is just one-sixth of the force felt here on Earth.'

'Exactly!' said Commander Margaret. 'And using the chair, you'll be able to experience what lower gravity on the moon feels like. I like to call this one the **Moon Walk Chair**. And just as with the Multi-Axis Trainer, this isn't a challenge – it is an experience.'

'I'm actually looking forward to this,' said Sally.

'And at least today we don't need to worry about another challenge being sabotaged,' Zoe said.

'Yeah, the only thing we have to worry about now is the Ghost King,' I said.

'You sound way too cheerful about that,' said Ralph.

☆ 🚀 ☆

The Moon Walk Chair hung suspended from the ceiling, with a rope behind it that the Space

Camp staff held on to which made sure that we didn't go flying up too high. It looked almost like a bungee chair, but way cooler.

'Sam, you can go first,' said Regina.

I was a **LITTLE** bit nervous about the Moon Walk Chair, especially after the power had gone out when I was on the Multi-Axis Trainer. But I didn't want anyone to know that so I just nodded. 'Only if that is okay with everyone else?' I said, hoping that someone would say that they **REALLY** wanted to go first.

Everyone else nodded too.

'Great! Super, *super*, **SUPER** great!' I said with as much enthusiasm as I could manage. 'I guess I'll show you all how it's done.'

I hoisted myself up on to the Moon Walk Chair. It was a little like sitting on a bike with my legs on either side of it, but with a seat belt

across my lap and my waist.

Even after being strapped in with the harness, the whole thing felt **MUCH** less secure than I would have liked.

'Go ahead and take a jump,' said Commander Margaret from behind me. She was holding on to the rope attached to the chair. With a deep breath I leaped as high as I could and went **FLYING** up in the air. My stomach did somersaults inside me and I really did feel almost weightless.

'Wooo!' I yelled. 'I'm moon-walking!'

I bounced and jumped and hopped like a space bunny all across the room. The rest of Team Blue cheered me on.

When my turn had ended, I was smiling so hard my cheeks hurt.

'You guys,' I said breathlessly, 'that was **AMAZING**.'

'Let me go next!' said Sally, pushing to the front of our group and clambering up on the Moon Walk Chair.

'Yippee!' she shouted as she took a flying leap. 'This is **SO** awesome!' She was smiling wider than I'd ever seen her smile. 'I love it!' She leaned forwards. 'Look at me!'

'Sally,' said Commander Margaret sharply from behind the chair, 'be careful!'

'I'm strapped in with a helmet on,' Sally said. 'What's the worst that can happen?' She did another big jump and as she came back down, she leaned forwards and put her arms out as if she was flying. As she did, her two long braids swept forwards over her shoulders, brushing the ground.

I saw what was going to happen an instant before it did. One of her braids snagged on an air vent in the floor. With her braid caught, Sally had tilted sideways, and she was yowling like a cat.

YOWWWL!

I dived forwards under the chair and quickly yanked her braid out of the air vent. A few hairs got caught, but most of it came out. As she was released, she flew back up into the air.

'Sam!' shouted Commander Margaret. 'Watch out!'

I rolled out from under the airborne chair just avoiding the seat before it came flying back down. Sally bounced a few more times, and then came down out of the chair and ran over to us. Commander Margaret followed.

'You saved my braid!' Sally said, a little breathlessly.

'I'd say he did more than that,' said Bernard. 'I'd say he saved you from certain doom!'

'I wouldn't go that far,' said Sally. 'But thank you. That was . . . really nice of you.'

'Sam,' said Commander Margaret, 'that was a very dangerous thing for you to do, but very brave.'

'We like to see **future astronauts** looking out for each other,' said Commander Wes.

'Yes,' said Commander Sharon, 'and ones who have excellent instinct and intuition.'

'When you're up in space, being able to depend on your fellow astronauts and trust your intuition could save your life,' said Commander Margaret. 'Now, while I don't want to encourage you to actively put yourself in danger, I do want to commend you for your bravery and quick thinking. So with that in mind, it is my pleasure to award Team Blue a bonus five points for Sam's brave actions.'

'Five points!' said Bernard. 'That means . . .
we could still win!'

'Good thing you have such long hair,' said
Ralph to Sally.

'Good thing Sam was so brave,' said Regina.

In that moment, I felt **braver** than I ever had.

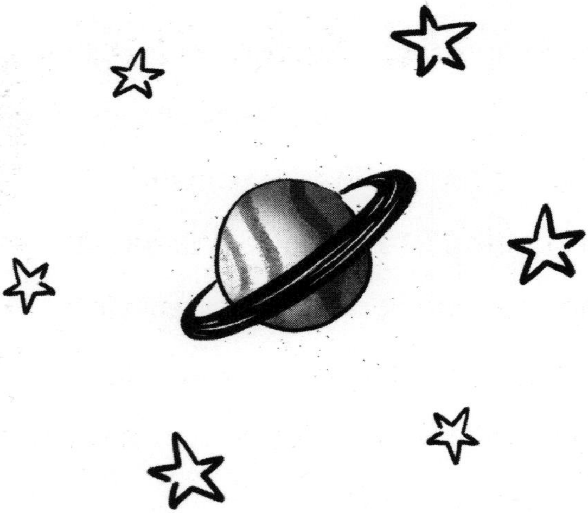

CHAPTER 16

THE REAL THIEF

All the rest of the day, my team and I couldn't stop smiling. We had a chance to win the whole competition!

I was still smiling when I got into my middle bunk that night. Bernard and Ralph were already in bed.

Then there was a sharp knock at the door. I sat up so quickly I hit my head on the top of the bunk.

'*Ow!*' I said, rubbing my head.

Bernard rolled out of his bottom bunk and opened the door a crack.

'Who's there?' he said, peering out.

'Open up and let us in!' said Zoe. 'We've got important new information.'

'About what?' said Bernard, still not opening the door. 'Is it more important than us getting a full night's sleep? Tomorrow is the final challenge! We all need to be well rested!'

LET US IN, BERNARD!

shouted Zoe.

Bernard opened the door.

Zoe, Regina and Sally came in. Zoe and Regina looked mad, and Sally had an odd expression on her face.

'Tell them, Sally,' said Zoe, crossing her arms. 'Tell them what you did.'

Sally looked down guiltily. 'I was going to give

everything back,' she said. 'I was just playing a little joke.'

'What little joke?' I asked.

SHE *is the one who* **STOLE** *from us!*

said Zoe.

'I dropped a book beneath the bunk beds, and when I went to get it, I found all our stuff,' explained Regina. She held out Ralph's watch, Bernard's pen and, best of all, my can of poison mist!

'My watch!' said Ralph, scrambling down from the top bunk.

'So . . . it wasn't the Ghost King,' I said slowly. 'It was **YOU**!'

'I was going to tell you,' said Sally, pouting. 'But then you

179

all got so excited thinking it was the Ghost King and made me feel like I was part of it, so . . . I didn't. I liked that it was all of us versus the Ghost King. I would have given everything back at the end of the week.'

'But why steal from us in the first place?' I said.

Sally sighed dramatically. 'How do you think I felt getting put on a team with a bunch of best friends?'

'Whoa,' said Ralph, looking up. 'We are definitely **NOT** all best friends.'

'You **OBVIOUSLY** are,' said Sally. 'You have all these inside jokes and all these stories. I didn't even want to come to Space Camp in the first place and I definitely didn't want to feel left out on the team that I was on.'

'We've been trying to include you,' said Regina.

'I'm sorry if you felt left out.'

'Well,' said Sally slowly, 'at first I did. That was why I sprayed Sam with the space food. And why I took your stuff. I thought it would make Space Camp a little more exciting for me. But then I started feeling like part of the team, and everything with the Ghost King happened, and then . . .' he looked up at me. 'Then Sam saved my braid. And that was when I realized I had to tell you all the truth. And I was going to tonight, I swear! But Regina found the stuff before I had a chance to.' She looked down again. 'I hope you guys can forgive me.'

'Why should we trust you?' said Ralph, putting his watch back on. 'You stole our most **PRIZED** possessions.'

'And you sabotaged our first mission,' said Zoe. 'We've given you plenty of chances!'

'Sam,' Bernard whispered to me, but in a very loud way that everyone heard, 'what are we going to do?'

I looked at Sally. 'You're a member of our crew whether you like it or not,' I said. 'And being part a crew means forgiving each other.'

'**WHAT?**' said Ralph. 'No way!'

'One time on **SPACE BLASTERS**,' I said, 'the alien Five-Eyed Frank stole space food from **Spaceman Jack** and **Captain Jane**, which meant they ran out of food on their space mission and had to do an emergency landing on Planet Bloop. And you know what? They forgave Five-Eyed Frank. Because he was part of their team.'

'This isn't a TV show, Sam,' said Zoe. 'This is **REAL** life.'

'I think what Sam is trying to say,' said Regina, 'is that Sally is part of our team, and even though she messed up, we should forgive her.'

'That's exactly it,' I said.

'I swear I'll make it up to you guys,' said Sally. 'I'll be **SO** good at the next challenge. I promise. And I won't steal from you again.'

'We're going to keep her on our crew, aren't we?' said Ralph, rolling his eyes.

'Looks like it,' said Zoe with a huff.

'At least now we don't need to worry about the Ghost King,' said Bernard.

'Well,' said Sally, 'that's the thing. Yes, I took your stuff, but what about the lights mysteriously going on and off? That wasn't me.'

'And something weird happened when we were walking over here,' said Regina. 'You know how the hall lights are motion sensor lights?'

We all nodded.

'Well, before we turned down your hallway,

the lights flickered on. And there was **NOBODY** there.'

I got goosebumps on the back of my neck. 'Let's watch,' I said. I cracked open the door just the tiniest bit. The corridor was dark.

'Nothing,' I said after a few moments of staring into the dark hallway.

And then the lights went on.

There was nobody there.

I quickly **SLAMMED** the door shut.

'You're right,' I said to Regina.

Regina nodded. 'The Ghost King is still on the loose at Space Camp.'

CHAPTER 17

SPACE RACE

'Regina!' said Ralph. 'You can't really believe that!'

'What else could it be?' said Regina.

'About a **MILLION** other things,' said Ralph.

But then the lights above us flickered on and off, on and off.

We all started yelling.

'IT'S THE GHOST KING!' I yelled.

'HE'S TRYING TO COMMUNICATE!' shouted Regina.

'OKAY, YOU'RE RIGHT, YOU'RE

RIGHT!' cried Ralph.

'DO YOU GUYS REALLY FORGIVE ME?' screamed Sally.

When the lights finally stopped flickering and we stopped yelling, we were all out of breath as if we'd just run a race.

'Okay,' I said, 'we forgive Sally, we're going to win the Space Camp competition and, most importantly, the Ghost King is **DEFINITELY** still here at Space Camp.'

☆ 🚀 ☆

'Good morning, cadets,' said Commander Margaret.

'Good morning, Commander Margaret,' everyone chanted back. I put my hand up to try to hide a yawn. I had **BARELY** slept that night. Every time a light had gone on in the hallway or I'd heard a noise, my eyes had flown open. I'd been convinced it was the Ghost King coming to get me at last.

'Your time at Space Camp is coming to a close. I hope you are all very proud of yourselves.' Commander Margaret smiled at us all. 'Now, before you depart tomorrow, you have one final challenge. The Space Race! Your team will race in a simulated mission from Earth to the International Space Station, which is **two hundred and fifty-four** miles above Earth and travels at about seventeen thousand miles per hour in a circular orbit around Earth. That is going to be difficult enough and you'll encounter various additional challenges along the way. Working together, there won't be anything you can't overcome. Are you ready?'

We all cheered.

'Then let's blast off to the moon!'

187

Each team went into their own spaceship simulator that had been designed like **REAL** spaceships that go to the International Space Station and **BEYOND**! In our official Space Camp uniforms, I really felt like we were about to blast off into space.

'Okay, Captain Sam,' said Ralph, 'what's the plan?'

I swelled with pride. 'Bernard, you're the chief engineer today, so can you start working out the calculations to get us going? Zoe and Regina, you'll drive the spaceship. Ralph and Sally, can you two be ready to handle anything that comes our way?'

'Got it, Captain!' said Bernard, starting to write down the maths.

Commander Margaret's voice came on over the intercom. 'Good luck, teams. We'll be watching to see how you work together and problem-solve.'

'We're ready for blast off, Captain Sam,' said Zoe.

As Zoe and Regina fired up the engine, the whole spaceship started to tremble. It was like when I went on the Astro Blast Simulator at the Space Museum, but **SO MUCH COOLER**! Plus, this time I had my friends with me, so I was **NOT** afraid.

'Everyone in position!' I said. 'Seat belts on!'

'Five, four, three, two, one . . . **BLAST OFF**!'

I looked out of the windows and, even though I knew the clouds hurtling past me were a simulation, I felt like I was leaving Earth behind and going out to explore the next frontier – outer space.

'We're in space,' said Ralph. 'And it looks like we've got a meteor coming in! Veer left!'

'On it,' said Regina, and the whole spaceship swerved.

'There's another spaceship coming up behind us,' said Sally, watching the monitor. 'I think it's Team Red.'

'Of course it's Team Red!' I said. 'Regina, Zoe, can we go any faster?'

'I think so,' said Regina.

'I can **ALWAYS** go faster,' said Zoe. She flipped a switch and the spaceship rumbled.

I scanned the monitor. Team Red was still right behind us.

'Sam,' said Bernard, 'if we're going to dock on to the International Space Station first, we've got to go **NOW**!'

'Regina, Zoe, you heard our engineer. Full blast!'

As the simulated stars flew by our windows, I wondered if one day I really would be leading a space mission.

'I see it!' shouted Zoe, looking at the screen. 'I see the International Space Station! But Team Red is gaining on us somehow!'

'Go past the space station and then hit the brakes!' shouted Bernard.

'Why would we go *past* the Space Station?' asked Regina.

'We want the International Space Station to catch us, not the other way around. We'll pull ahead of it, and then turn around. Right now, we are orbiting around Earth four minutes faster than Space Station, so we're slowly catching up to it. Just as we pass it, we need to hit the brakes and do a U-turn, and then when the Space Station catches back up to us, we'll fire

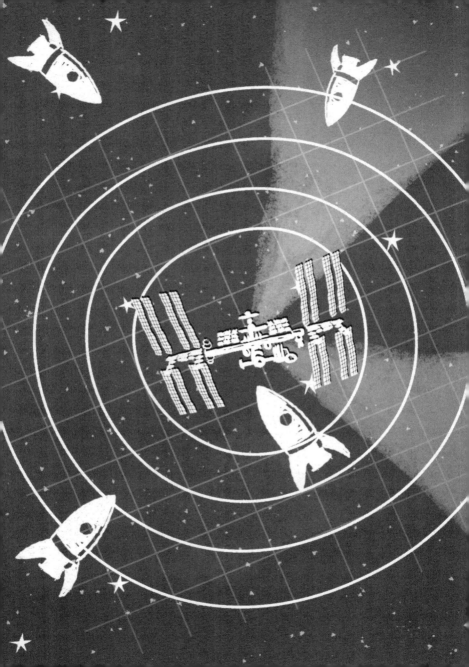

the engines once more, and dock.[1] It's all about precision, and Team Red is just focusing on speed!'

'Good thinking, Bernard!' I said as Team Red's spaceship flew past us. I held my breath as their spaceship approached the Space Station first, but instead of docking, they shot right past it!

'They were going too fast and overshot,' said Bernard with a smile. 'But no time for celebration, now we need to U-turn and dock!'

'Roger that,' said Zoe as she hit the brakes and whipped the spaceship around.

I got on the intercom. 'International Space Station, this is Team Blue, ready for landing. International Space Station, do you copy?'

---

[1] This is how real astronauts land on the International Space Station!

'Team Blue, we copy,' said a voice (I was pretty sure it was Commander Wes). 'Dock A is ready to receive your ship.'

'Team Blue incoming,' I said.

'Whoa,' said Ralph, his eyes wide. 'How did you learn how to talk like a real astronaut?'

'**SPACE BLASTERS** of course,' I said.

With precision and focus, Zoe and Regina manoeuvred our spaceship on to the loading dock. The intercom crackled to life again.

'Congratulations, Team Blue, you are the first to arrive on the International Space Station!'

CHAPTER 18

I SMELL A RAT

I couldn't believe that our team had won the Space Race!

After all the teams had successfully reached the International Space Station, we joined the Space Camp commanders in Area One. 'Well done, Team Blue,' said Commander Margaret with a big smile. 'Your teamwork paid off!'

'I'd like to especially commend Cadet Bernard for his quick calculations which helped Team Blue successfully dock at the International Space Station,' said Commander Wes.

'It's just a stupid simulation,' said Felix, rolling

his eyes. 'If it had been real life, we definitely would have beaten them.'

'I don't know about that,' said Commander Sharon. 'Bernard was absolutely right about the need for a spaceship to be orbiting around Earth four minutes faster than the International Space Station.'

Bernard simultaneously beamed and turned bright red at all the public praise.

'Everyone did a wonderful job,' said Commander Margaret. 'We've tallied all the points and the overall winner of the Space Camp competition is . . . **TEAM BLUE**!'

My whole team started jumping in the air and hugging and screaming. We were the winners of it all! Even with two of our challenges being sabotaged, we'd managed to win!

'Please come up to receive your winning pin

badges,' said Commander Wes.

We all lined up and stood proudly as the Space Camp commanders presented us with our winning pins.

'Now smile for your picture,' said Commander Sharon. 'This will be going up on the Winner's Wall with all the previous Space Camp winning teams.'

I was so happy I almost couldn't stand it. My whole body was fizzing with excitement and pride.

The only thing that could have made it better was if **Spaceman Jack** and **Captain Jane** had been there.

After all the excitement of the ceremony, I went back to our sleep-pod room by myself to have a moment alone. As much as I loved spending time with my friends and my space crew, I just wanted some privacy to look at my special Space Camp winner's badge. It was blue and shaped like a shield, with gold stars and a white spaceship on it.

I looked at myself in the mirror, still in my official Space Camp uniform, wearing my shiny winner's badge. Feeling a little silly, I did the **SPACE BLASTERS** 'for the universe' salute to myself.

As I did, I knocked off my badge and it fell

behind the little chest of drawers in front of the mirror.

'Oh no!'

I quickly got down on my hands and knees to see if I could find it. And as I did, the lights flickered. I got goosebumps on my arms. I was alone in my room and the Ghost King was on the loose. For all I knew, he might have even been in my room with me!

My first instinct was to get up and run. But I couldn't leave without my winner's badge.

I pushed the chest of drawers away.

And gasped.

Behind the chest of drawers was a **HUGE HOLE** in the wall.

And staring right at me with beady red eyes as it gnawed on some exposed wires was a giant <u>**RAT**</u>. I yelled and scrambled backwards.

The rat stayed where it was and continued to chew on the wires. I wished my trusty sidekick, my pet snake Fang, were here! Fang would have been able to catch the rat in an instant.

As I stared at the rat biting down on one of the wires, the lights above me flickered. And all of a sudden I realized that this rat was the Ghost King!

I had to catch it to show everyone! I suddenly had a brilliant idea. I jumped up and grabbed Bernard's not-so-secret tin of chocolates he kept under his pillow. Then I emptied out the nearest suitcase (it happened to be Ralph's), put a chocolate in it, and put it next to the hole.

Then I waited.

I didn't have to wait long. The rat sniffed and scrambled into the suitcase. I reached out and slammed the lid shut – with only a little bit of a shudder. The rat squeaked and ran around, making scratching noises on the inside of the suitcase, so I knew it was fine. Plus it had a chocolate.

I grabbed my pin badge, proudly put it back on, and went to tell everybody what I'd discovered.

CHAPTER 19

SPACEMAN SAM

The Space Camp commanders were **VERY** impressed. And Bernard and Zoe couldn't believe I'd caught the rat on my own. Sally asked if she could take the rat home and keep it as a pet.

Ralph was a little mad I'd used his suitcase to trap the rat, and snorted a bit when I told him it was for the good of the crew **AND** for all of Space Camp. But then he reluctantly gave me a high five for solving the mystery of the Ghost King at Space Camp.

'I still think the Ghost King might be on the loose,' said Regina. I nodded.

'You never can tell with the Ghost King,' I said. 'He's a tricky one.' This is what **Spaceman Jack** always says.

To thank me for figuring out why the lights had been flickering, the Space Camp commanders gave me a second pin badge! 'That was a very brave thing of you to do,' said Commander Wes as my team crowded around me cheering.

'For the universe!' we all shouted as we flung our hands up in the **SPACE BLASTERS** salute.

'I think you've got a real future as an astronaut, Sam,' said Commander Margaret as she shook my hand.

And maybe one day I really will go to space, just like **Spaceman Jack** and **Captain Jane**.

But until then, I've got my own crew here on Earth.

And no matter what we have to face, I am **<u>NOT</u>** afraid!

Katie and Kevin are definitely <u>NOT</u> afraid of answering some author questions ❗

We can't believe this is Sam's sixth adventure! What is your favourite thing about going on adventures with Sam and his friends?

Katie: I love when the crew is all together on an exciting mission and they use their codenames they came up with in *Sam Wu is NOT Afraid of the Dark*. And I love when they wear ridiculous outfits like they do in *Zombies*. And most of all I love when they work together to overcome an obstacle or fear and have fun while doing it.

Kevin: I love how Sam acts brave even when he might be a little bit nervous and how he is willing to do anything for his friends.

After reading this book, we are TOTALLY desperate to visit Space Camp – have you guys been?

Kevin: I wanted to go to Space Camp SO MUCH when I was a kid, but I never got a chance to go. So sending Sam to Space Camp was total wish fulfilment for me!

Katie: I never went to Space Camp either but I had so much fun researching Space Camp for this book! The only kind of camps I went to as a kid were outdoor nature ones.

We were definitely NOT scared when Sam got into the SPACE CHAIR that goes UPSIDE DOWN. Which Space Camp activity would be your favourite?

Katie: Definitely the Moon Walk Chair!

Kevin: All of it! Hanging out with real astronauts would be awesome.

If you had to have a meal in space tubes, what would you eat?

Katie: Probably mashed potatoes because they are already mushy!

Kevin: Yuck! No thank you. But if I had to . . . definitely pizza! I bet even space tube pizza tastes pretty good.

Now you are total space experts, would you like to go into actual space?

Katie: I don't know if I'd want to go into actual real life space (I'd miss my life here on Earth too much!) but I love writing about it! Hopefully we can keep adventuring through our books!

Kevin: I used to think I wanted to be an astronaut, but now I think I might be too scared to go into space. I do really love space though, so I want to keep writing about Spaceman Jack and Captain Jane's adventures – who knows what they'll get up to next . . .